MW00791317

FALL FOR *Me*

LEXI KINGSTON

Published by L. Kingston Books, LLC
Edited by Elaine York, Allusion Publishing
Cover Design by Kari March Designs

FALL FOR ME

To the girls whose best friend feels like home.

Chapter One

"LAINEY BROKE UP WITH ME."

My teeth close around a long stick of licorice as I balance my laptop on my knees and clench my phone between my ear and shoulder. A soft breeze floats up from the ocean and tickles the wind chimes hanging on the porch of my family's vacation home.

"Lainey? Really?" I ask with my mouth full. "I could have sworn she had wedding bells for eyes."

Beckett's love life has been a revolving door of women this past year, and every single one of them has broken up with him. He always inadvertently does something to push them away, and you can call him commitment-phobic or just plain disinterested, but the man can't keep a girl longer than a couple of weeks—a month, *tops,* if she's generous enough to overlook his initial red flags in the hope that his good looks will make up for them.

Lainey was the perfect girl for him. She checked

every single one of his boxes—classic beauty with a hint of nerd to balance out her perfection, gorgeous blonde hair, and the bluest eyes I've ever seen. I only ever spoke to her over the phone when she was with Beckett, but she seemed genuine.

She was everything any sane man would want in a woman, and yet he drove her away.

"That's the problem. She did. But apparently, I'm 'not the commitment type,' and she 'can't condone spending any more time in a relationship that's standing still.' Can you believe that bullshit? I really thought this one would last, Mac."

"Yes." I laugh, shaking my head. It's hard to be sympathetic when this is the third girl to dump him in just over a month. "I *can* believe it because you *are* afraid of commitment."

"I am not," he argues, sounding offended. "We only dated for two weeks, and she dumped me before I could get to know her. How am I expected to commit to a serious relationship?"

I withhold my honest opinion because he sounds distressed. With every breakup, he grows more and more frustrated with his love life, and no matter how many times I give him advice, he doesn't listen.

I sigh and set my laptop aside, finishing the piece of licorice I've been eating so I can give him my full attention. "Tell me—what did you actually like about her?"

Silence.

The wind chimes dance and sing their soothing

2

melody as I wait for him to come up with even the most basic thing he liked about Lainey. And as I suspected, he has nothing. "My point exactly. You *didn't* like her. Girls can totally sense that, you know."

"Hey, I wasn't done thinking," he argues. "Lainey was... she was... she had..." He curses under his breath. "Her smile was nice! Yeah, and... she had... silky brown hair... and she, uh..."

"This is painful to listen to—wait. Brown hair? I thought Lainey was blonde?" I ask, suddenly confused about the ex-in-question.

"You're thinking of Lacey," he corrects, and I'm taken aback.

Lacey?

"Then who the hell is Lainey? And what happened to Lacey?"

"She dumped me a few days before I met Lainey because she said I..."

"Couldn't commit?" I supply, smirking.

"Nah," he says easily, a smile in his voice. "She said I was too sexy to be seen with her in public. She didn't want to drag me down."

We both know if that's what she said, he wouldn't have hesitated to finish his sentence.

"I don't think I've met Lainey, then."

"That's probably for the best," he admits sheepishly. "I don't think you would have liked her."

I bet I would have liked her more than you.

I bite back that retort because, again, he seems upset. "Why not?"

He hesitates for a moment. "She was a bit snotty—and before you say anything, I know how you feel about bitchy girls, but she's really nice underneath it all."

I roll my eyes. *I'm sure she is.*

Beckett's girlfriends all have two things in common if nothing else: they're smoking hot and tend to despise me.

"That's called being fake, Beckett. It's a true art form that most modern girls have mastered to feel superior and distance themselves from any *meaningful* interactions."

"Don't start," he begs, and I realize I'm squeezing the bag of licorice so tightly in my lap that a few of them have fused from the heat.

"Sorry, I'm done," I relent. The lack of respect and consideration most people hold for anyone but themselves has only further vexed me as I've gotten older. First, it's talking behind your back and spreading false rumors in middle school, then it's excluding you from parties and making plans without you in high school. Not to mention the shame that's cast when you opt not to attend college post-graduation. Same story, a hundred different friends.

If Lainey is anything like she sounds, I'm sure I would have hated her.

"Will you just come home already?" Beckett asks, yanking me out of my thoughts. I can't help but laugh at the child-like pleading in his voice. "I can't wallow in my misery while eating ice cream and watching *The Choice* alone."

"You absolutely can, it's just less pathetic when I'm in the room," I point out, biting my lip with a grin. I pick at the blue polish on my fingernails, which, when asked, Beckett said would be the perfect color for vacation because it matches the ocean. He's such an idiot, but I know if he were here, I wouldn't be sitting on the porch alone while my parents and brother argued inside over where to eat for dinner. He'd have me laughing so hard we'd drown out their raised voices. "Besides, I'll be home in a few days. I can wallow with you then."

"A few days too long," he insists, then his voice drops an octave, coming out quieter. "I miss you."

I bite my lip, staring at my nails. "Me, too."

Waves crash in the distance, and I breathe in the humid, salty air, hating his ability to get my heart pounding with three words.

"Mac, we're leaving!" Mom bellows from inside, startling me.

I close my eyes, gritting my teeth.

"Rough day?" Beckett asks, sympathetic.

I snort. "Rough day? Try rough *week*. I don't know why we bother with family vacations when we'd all rather be anywhere else."

To make matters worse, Mom's tone just now wasn't one that meant they came to a peaceful agreement on where to eat. Instead, it indicates the fight isn't nearly over, and whatever they were arguing about—in this case, a restaurant—will likely resurface later. Unfortunately for me, "later" typically entails some sort of public humiliation on my end while my parents trade insults and our waiter weakly asks if we need another minute to look over the menu.

"You could always ditch the family and fly home to me," he jokes, though I'm not entirely sure he's kidding.

We've been best friends forever, but now that he's in Boston for school and I'm floundering into my second gap year, summer is the only time we see each other besides the occasional weekend and holiday. This year, however, Beckett had to complete a summer internship before his senior year, and my family's annual vacation overlapped with his arrival home. Meaning, I haven't seen him in the better part of four months.

"Only if you pay for my flight," I tease, knowing that he can hardly afford his off-campus apartment right now. His class schedule doesn't allow much time for a job, and his internship was unpaid, so he's more broke than usual. Interestingly enough, he's majoring in finance.

"MacKenzie!" Mom yells, this time from the driveway.

With an inhale, I lean forward to close my laptop and seal the bag of licorice.

"Ouch—full name? That can't be good."

"Never is." I set my stuff inside and grab my purse off the counter, then twist the lock before closing the back door. "I'll talk to you soon."

"Bye, Mac."

I end the call and jog around the house on a walkway so covered in sand that you can hardly see the pavers anymore. Two palm trees sway on either side of the gate I push open, and I glance over my shoulder at the crystal-clear water that stretches farther than I can see.

My family is waiting for me in the rental car, and the cool air conditioner smothers me in a tundra the moment I slide into the back seat. My parents are up front, my brother is in the seat opposite mine, and his wife Angela is in the last row with their two kids.

Ryan is thirteen years older than me and lives in Oklahoma with his family—quite the distance from where we grew up in Richlynd, West Virginia, right along the border of Pennsylvania. We've never been close because of our age gap, and by the time I was old enough to bond with him, he'd already settled down to make a life for himself.

I know he never meant to abandon me, but he wanted to escape our parents' arguing so badly that he left for law school and never looked back. I understand, and yet, part of me resents him for it. Mostly though, I'm indifferent. It's hard to be mad at someone you don't know the first thing about.

With his job, wife, and two kids keeping him busy, he doesn't have much time to visit Richlynd, where my parents and I still live, and he spends most holidays with his in-laws. This is the only time of year we can force him to take off work to acknowledge our existence.

"Where are we going?" I ask lightly, so as not to induce another argument. I pull my long hair out of the bun it's been in all afternoon and work out the kinks, digging around in the passenger seat pocket for the hat I left after breakfast. The bill is slightly bent, so I flex the material a few times before placing it on my head.

"Some Italian joint," Angela says when no one else

bothers to respond. She's tending to the kids in the back seat while they whine profusely about their hunger.

I give her a tiny smile as a thanks for being the only person to acknowledge I'd spoken, but she's too preoccupied to notice.

My dad presses down on the gas pedal, launching us out of the driveway and narrowly missing a mailbox. He comes to a stop at the end of our road, and with a raised eyebrow, glances at my mom. He scratches the gray and black scruff on his face, then rubs his fingers along his chin impatiently.

"What now?" she gripes, pulling down the visor and applying a fresh coat of concealer under her eyes to mask her dark circles. I'm not sure if her makeup is running due to the heat or from crying, but either way, after a few swipes of her finger, it's like it was never there.

His face seems to shorten as he clenches his jaw. "Where are we going?"

Mom slams the visor back into place without so much as glancing at him. "I don't know, maybe you should have put the address in the GPS before running down the neighbor's mailbox in haste."

Angela clears her throat. "I think if you turn right at the next stop sign—"

"*You're the passenger,*" Dad says, as though it was common sense for Mom to have already programmed the directions. "*You* picked the restaurant. The damn near least you could do is tell me how to get there."

No one acknowledges Angela's kind attempt to tell him where to go.

My nose burns slightly as the air settles, and I look around curiously. Rental cars always have a sort of *odor*. Not dirty and grimy, yet not clean. You can tell someone else has been there before you and left behind remnants of their presence—faded stains on the carpet, a rip in the seat fabric, or my personal favorite, the brown mystery goop on the ceiling.

That's not, however, what I smell today.

Someone reeks of stale booze—probably the cheap whiskey we found in the closet our first night here—and it's intensified by the humidity since the air conditioner isn't nearly strong enough to combat the South Carolina heat.

I glance at my brother, who has his head in his hands and his knees propped on his elbows. I vaguely remember him getting car sick a lot when I was younger, but I'm pretty positive it's a hangover that's making him nauseous now.

Our parents' voices gradually escalate, and it won't be long until they start screaming again.

We just have to wait for Dad to raise his voice because that means any apprehensions about fighting in front of us are gone.

"You know," Ryan says, rubbing his hands down his face. "I'm going to order in."

He gets out of the car and stretches while Angela unbuckles Eli and Emory, then starts walking the four blocks to the house, me close behind.

"What's going on?" Eli tugs on his mom's pant leg. Emory is in her arms, voicing similar questions.

Angela brushes the hair off his forehead. "We're going to eat at home tonight."

Eli groans. "*Again?* I wanted meatballs."

She merely sighs.

Inside, Angela makes craft Mac n' Cheese for the kids, Ryan uncorks a new bottle of Jack Daniel's, and I order myself a pizza and take it up to my room when it arrives.

Closing the door, I climb on my bed and pull the large pizza box onto my lap before turning on the TV. I navigate to the streaming services while simultaneously making a call.

"You just can't function without me, can you?" Beckett answers on the fourth ring.

I lean into the sea of pillows propped against my headboard, then rip off a large hunk of pizza before responding. "I was afraid you'd feel like less of a man if you cried over *The Choice* alone."

He huffs a laugh, and I take another bite of pizza, relishing the flavor as I bite into a juicy banana pepper. "What happened to dinner?"

"We didn't even make it to the main road."

Beckett is quiet for a moment. "Where's Ryan and his wife?"

I set down my pizza, suddenly not hungry anymore. "They made their own dinner."

"And they didn't offer you any?" he asks, floored.

"There wasn't enough for me anyway."

"I don't give a shit how much there was, they should have offered," he gripes, and his fury takes some of the edge off my disappointment. Just knowing someone cares enough to be angry for me makes me feel better.

"It doesn't matter. You up for a long-distance movie?" I ask, changing the subject. "My room has a smart TV; I can stream anything."

Whenever Beckett doesn't have a mound of homework, he calls me from school so we can catch up and watch movies together. But with his internship and my job at the diner back home, we haven't done that in a while.

"Always. It's my turn to pick, though."

"No, it's not," I argue, distinctly remembering the last time he had a say in what we watched. He chose a horror movie, and I couldn't sleep with the light off for weeks.

"I watch your Nicholas Sparks movies; you can watch something I like."

"Fine, but please don't pick anything that will give me nightmares. I'm begging you."

I hear the clicking of a remote on his end, and after a few minutes, he tells me to put on a movie called *This Means War*.

"Will it make me want to hide in the closet?" I ask, not entirely trusting him.

He chuckles. "No. It's an action movie, but there's some romance in it for you."

I smile, teeth snagging my bottom lip. "Sounds like a fair trade."

He counts down from five, and we press play at the same time. I set the pizza box aside after finishing my piece, then pick up another, occasionally talking to Beckett about the plotline between bites.

Halfway through the movie, I doze off to the sound of his voice on the other end of the line.

The next few days go just like the first four did: nonsensical arguing, licorice for lunch, and leftover pizza for dinner. Very little family bonding occurs, and when we see my brother off at the airport, I'm honestly relieved.

My parents and I head to our gate, and when we find seats, they sit on either side of me so I act as a buffer between their latest disagreement.

As I'm about to make an excuse for the bathroom, my phone vibrates in my hand with a text from Beckett.

Beckett: *Beer o'clock starts now.*

I roll my eyes as a follow-up message appears at the base of the screen, consisting of cheersing beer bottles and a picture of the folding chair on the balcony outside my bedroom.

Me: *You're an idiot. My plane doesn't board for another hour. You're going to be drinking alone for a while. Also, care to explain how you managed to get onto my balcony?*

My bedroom is on the second floor of our house; besides climbing a twelve-foot ladder, I have no idea how he possibly could have gotten up there.

He's also lucky my neighbors know him, or they might have called the police.

A second picture appears of the tree beside my window. He drew a stick figure climbing up it, latching onto the windowsill, and jumping onto the balcony.

Me: *I amend my previous statement; you're not an idiot.*
Beckett: *Thank you.*
Me: *You're a dumbass.*
Beckett: *That hurts.*

"I spoke with Anna Jenkins this morning," Mom says out of the blue, raising an assuming eyebrow.

Here we go.

Shifting uncomfortably in my seat, I clench my phone in my hand and cross my knees.

"And?" I implore when she continues to stare at me like we're both in on the same dirty secret. She leans in slightly, as though it's imperative no one overhears what she says next.

"Don't play coy with me." She winks, eyelashes coated with a thick glob of mascara that darkens her already sunken-in eyes. She used to be a smoker, and even though she claims she hasn't touched a cigarette since the day I was born, the lingering smell of smoke on her clothes tells me she still sneaks the occasional hit when she's stressed.

So, all the time.

When it's clear she's not going to elaborate or let whatever this is go, I say, "I have no idea what you're getting at."

She sighs before saying what she thinks is the most exciting piece of information I'll ever hear.

Spoiler alert: it's not.

"Tony broke up with his girlfriend." Her smile grows large and toothy as she bumps her shoulder into mine.

"So?"

"Now, Tony wouldn't tell her anything," she says, lowering her voice, "but Anna thinks they broke up because he's still in love with *you*."

I withhold an eye roll.

Tony Jenkins and I dated for over a year and broke up because we were both, to put it plainly, really bored of each other. It was a mutual decision with no residual feelings involved. We even had a few classes together before we graduated, and the awkwardness was nonexistent. In fact, we chose to work together on our final project so we wouldn't have to worry about other group members failing to carry their weight.

"Tony went to Penn State, and his girlfriend is at Yale. I think distance has more to do with that breakup than me. Besides," I press on when she doesn't look convinced, "I'm not interested in him anyway. We broke up for a reason. There was nothing there anymore."

She shakes her head, and her big blonde curls

bounce stiffly, glued together with enough hairspray to bump Super Glue down on the list of best adhesives. "You haven't so much as looked at another man since the two of you broke up. Maybe there's a reason for that. Breakups can be hard, Mac. You just have to—"

"Please, stop," I beg tiredly, praying for the swift death of this conversation.

She puts her hands up defensively. "All I'm saying is that you spend so much time either in your room or with Beckett that you haven't allowed yourself to branch out and meet new people."

I want to tell her that's what college is for; however, bringing up the prospect of more school makes me nauseous. I barely survived the hell that was my high school—I'm not exactly eager to spend four more years judged by my academic standing, social popularity, and whatever other aspects of schooling that won't mean a rat's ass after graduation.

I'd rather people think I'm a recluse.

"I meet people at the diner all the time," I argue.

She sits me with a dry look. "I meant people under fifty and over eighteen. When we get home, I think you need to call Tony. Check in to see how he's doing—you never know where it could lead."

"I'm not doing that," I grit, praying she doesn't ambush me with some dinner with him and his family. It wouldn't be the first time she tried to trap me in a room with whatever man she thought would be good for me at the time.

She huffs. "And why not?"

"Because I am seeing someone," I lie, and as much guilt as I feel, I'd rather mislead her than get stuck in another stuffy dining room with someone I have no interest in.

She turns on me instantly, eyes bulging out of her head.

I hold up a hand, stopping her before she can hound me with questions. Then I think of the best way to give her information about my relationship without actually telling her anything about this fictitious man. "I'm not sure where it's going yet, so for now, I'd rather not talk about it and jinx us, okay?"

She purses her lips and nods, forcibly holding herself back for my benefit. Despite her accusations, she's not entirely wrong about my love life—or lack thereof.

Every time I meet a man I find remotely attractive, it's like my brain puts up a roadblock with a ten-foot sign that reads "not what I'm looking for" before I so much as learn his name.

I used to think there was something wrong with me. That maybe my parents' dysfunctional relationship ruined me for emotional attachments. Then sometimes I wonder if it's not some external force, but *someone* whose attention I crave more than anyone else's.

My stomach twists at the absurd thought, and I push it to the farthest corners of my mind.

Now *that's* ridiculous.

Just because Beckett is the only man I want to spend time with doesn't mean anything. His friendship is merely a solace I never imagined I'd need so desperately in my life—like a replacement older brother since mine couldn't be bothered. He's two years older than me, but even when he graduated and I was still in high school, our relationship never suffered—he made sure of it.

Beckett is my constant, and he may go through girl after girl, but *I'm* the one who has always been there. That's how I know there's no possible way he's the reason I won't let myself open up to anyone else. Our friendship is too precious. Not to mention, he has never looked at me as anything more than who I am—his snarky, quirky, romance-movie-loving best *friend*. If there's anything I'm certain of, it's that.

He'd chase a million random girls to the ends of the Earth and back again, but never me.

He'd never fall for me.

Chapter Two

BECKETT ISN'T on my balcony when I get home like I'd hoped.

He left behind three beer cans for me to throw away, either too lazy to take them home, or because he wanted to give me an excuse to text him the second I got here.

He knows I can't resist the urge to bitch him out for being lazy.

> **Me:** *You use my balcony to drink because your dad would kick your ass if he caught you slacking on the yard work... yet you leave all of the evidence for MY parents to find. Your logic = nonexistent.*
> **Beckett:** *I can't tell if you're joking or genuinely mad.*

I consider screwing with him, but I'm too exhausted from the flight to utilize the sort of mental manipulation that accompanies pranking him.

Me: *Joking. Trust me, your black eye would know if I wasn't.*

The bubbles indicating he's typing pop up on the bottom of the screen, then disappear and reappear before he responds.

Beckett: *Cute. So, my parents' twenty-fifth anniversary is coming up, and I want to do something nice for them, but I'm not sure what. Want to hit the mall and help a guy out?*
Me: *My presence wouldn't have anything to do with you having three beers under your belt and being unable to drive, would it?*
Beckett: *Four. I carried the last one home. And no. Your presence is mandatory.*

Exhaustion suddenly nowhere to be found, I change out of my airplane clothes and match a pair of jean shorts with a front-tying crop top. The neckline is a little lower than I'm used to, but the cut shows off my Carolina glow, so I don't mind. My hair is blonder from the sun, too, and it falls in loose, messy waves down my back, framing my round face.

Grabbing my keys, I jog downstairs, past the kitchen, and out the front door.

Six minutes later, I'm parked outside Beckett's house and honking my horn in our traditional hurry-your-ass-up salute. My Jeep's windows are rolled down, the air conditioner is off, and the longer I sit here with the sticky air suffocating me, the more anxious I am to see him.

Our distance felt different this year. We always talk while he's away, but not as much as we have recently. Every time I checked my phone in the last week there was a new message from him. We usually spend every day together otherwise, so it shouldn't be weird, but vacations have always been the one or two weeks a year that we have little contact.

Nothing has changed. Absolutely nothing. Yet, everything feels different.

My eyes are glued to the door on the left of the garage, painted a bright shade of white that matches the shudders on his parents' house beside it. Beckett moved into the apartment above their detached garage a little less than a year ago to have more freedom when he comes home. He lives by himself at Boston College, so I'm sure he's grown to value his time alone. Though for the life of me, I can't fathom why. His family is perfect. If I grew up in his household, I'd never leave.

My breath hitches when I see movement behind a dirty window, and a moment later, the door swings open and Beckett steps outside wearing a light blue button-down that's only clasped a quarter of the way up his stomach. Keys dangle from his fingers, and he jiggles the door handle to ensure it locks behind him.

Then he's walking toward my car in effortless strides, crossing the sidewalk to cut through the grass, broad shoulders and toned stomach catching my gaze as he moves. When he sees me, a tiny smirk plays on his tanned face that puts my vacation glow to shame.

Working in the sun every day has done him good.

Beckett does lawn work when he's home for the summers, and to say it's done his body many favors is an understatement.

My eyes drift to my tiny shirt that reveals most of my chest and stomach, and I suddenly regret not putting on a baggy t-shirt.

Or self-tanner.

Or doing more sit-ups.

I shake my head, ridding the self-consciousness from my mind.

Beckett knew me through braces and bangs, so I don't know why I'm freaking out about a tan that I wouldn't have on my best day.

Two blue eyes bore into mine as he nears the Jeep, and the moment he does, his hand slides over the leather interior until his fingers connect with the unlock button, promptly opening my door.

"Tell me you're not just going to sit there after disappearing on me?" he asks, grabbing me around the waist and hoisting me out of the vehicle before I can respond.

I loop my arms around his neck, and he spins me in a half circle before setting me on my feet and giving my shoulders a light squeeze. My arms slide down his biceps, and I stare up at him without a thought in my head.

He watches me like I'm supposed to say something,

and well, I suppose I should, considering I haven't yet, but my skin is still tingling from where he held me, and my tongue feels thick in my throat.

This isn't like me. Beckett hugs me all the time, so why does this feel so different?

Correction. Why am *I* so different all of a sudden?

Beckett is the same funny, sexy, teddy-bear-hearted boy I've known my entire life. The same boy who went off to college every fall for the past several years and came home in the summer.

His looks have never affected me before—or at least, they haven't affected me this way in a long time. I saw *him* through his braces and bowl-cut phase, and that's pretty much the only way I've ever let myself see him.

My throat bobs when I swallow.

Until today.

Good Lord. I feel like I'm melting, and not from the sun—unless the way it glistens off his tan skin counts. Because then I'm absolutely melting from the sun.

"Mac?" Beckett says my name, but it doesn't fully register. All I can do is stare at his familiar face, which is suddenly so foreign. It's like I'm seeing his dimpled, lady-killer smile and wavy blonde hair the way all the girls who drool over him do.

Except, I am *not* one of those girls.

Beckett was always cute, but he's only become more attractive with age—muscles pronounced, smile deadlier, and eyes more striking than my simple mind can comprehend.

Then he punches my arm in the most playful,

friendly way ever, and the allusion is shattered. "Earth to MacKenzie?"

"Right. Sorry. Hi!" I punch him back, then loop my arms around his neck in another hug, which he returns immediately. I hold my breath so as not to get a whiff of his sweet-smelling cologne and lose myself in a haze of ludicrous thoughts.

"You okay?" He rocks us back and forth and slides his hands across my back, tightening his grip before pulling back to search my gaze. "Not to sound full of myself, but you're usually more excited to see me."

I roll my eyes and step out of his grasp, shifting the sunglasses atop my head to my nose like a shield between me and his hypnotic eyes.

"Long flight," I explain, gesturing toward the car and taking a step backward. "Ready to go?"

"I'll drive." He nods, pocketing his house keys as I hoist myself onto the seat. He slides in beside me and closes the door as I scoot across the bench seat to the passenger side. The door has been stuck for years, and since Beckett is the only person who ever gets in my car, I've never seen a reason to pay the money to have it fixed.

I raise an eyebrow as he buckles his seatbelt. "Wait, weren't you drinking earlier?"

He glances at me, tongue slipping between his lips as he works up a response. "The picture I sent you earlier was actually taken yesterday. I didn't have time to head over to your place today."

"So, you just trespass on my balcony whenever you

feel like it?" I slap his arm, and he pretends to be offended.

"I missed you, sue me."

"I don't believe you. Let me smell your breath," I say, even though I do, in fact, believe that he would climb up my balcony to drink beer for the hell of it.

He leans toward me, eyes sparkling with mischief as he huffs in my general direction. I take an overdramatized inhale, smelling nothing but the mint-flavored gum in his mouth, but before I can relay the verdict, he says, "You know, you could always kiss me to be sure."

My cheeks burn hot, and I shove him absurdly, trying to play off his comment like it doesn't completely light me on fire inside. "Screw off."

He chuckles, satisfied with himself as I fasten my seatbelt. Then he shifts the car into drive and takes off down the hill. The wind whips through the windows, bringing with it smells of grass and flowers that mingle with the musky scent of Beckett's skin. The smoke from countless grills tickles my nose as well, and I focus on that sensation, as opposed to the ones Beckett elicits within me.

If only he knew how much that one sentence derailed me. How, if he really tried to kiss me, I don't know that I'd push him away.

He says things like that all the time—it's good-humored sarcasm for us—so, for the love of God, why does the idea suddenly make my lips tingle with anticipation?

"So, I was thinking a candlelit dinner by the pool," Beckett says, and my head jerks around.

"What?" I ask, trying my best to sound casual and not at all short of breath. "I thought we were going to the mall."

"For my parents' anniversary..." He glances at me with a bewildered look on his face. "Are you sure you're okay?"

"Of course." I clear my throat, shifting on the seat.

He glances at me again, and I can tell he doesn't believe me.

"It's nothing, really," I assure him, covering my behavior with fragments of the truth. "I'm just distracted. My family fought the entire trip, and on the flight back, my mom started in on me about being single and antisocial."

"Shit. Again?" he asks, sympathetic. This isn't the first time my mother has pushed me to start dating again. The only difference is that this time she has someone in mind. *Tony*.

The last thing I need is our moms ganging up and forcing us on a date we won't enjoy.

"Unfortunately." I scrunch my nose. "So, I'm mentally drained and completely off my game. Forgive me?"

"There's nothing to forgive." Beckett reaches across the middle seat to squeeze my knee, and I tear my eyes from the blur of green outside to look at him.

His eyes are on the road, but I can tell something is

bugging him by the set of his jaw. "What about you? Have you talked to Lainey since the breakup?"

He gnaws on his bottom lip, clearly working up the courage to ask me something.

Beckett always has to find the right words when he wants to confide in someone, and knowing him, he spent all morning pondering how best to explain whatever's on his mind.

"Do you think she's right? Am I a commitment phobe?"

I hesitate. "Is that what she called you?"

He clears his throat, thumbs drumming the steering wheel to a country radio station playing faintly in the background. "Not in so many words, but I show up, right? Isn't that what a boyfriend is supposed to do?"

"Are you asking me if you're a good boyfriend?" I ask dryly, and I swear he cringes, but he covers it up so fast I think I might have imagined the reaction. "Look, all I know is that you're a great friend. You always have my back, and you have the unflinching ability to do things that most guys would grunt and groan about."

"Like helping you pick out a shade of nail polish," he points out, gesturing to my nails.

"Precisely. Now, do you freak out every time a girl tries to get serious with you... yeah, a little, but it's usually because you're already looking for a reason to dump her and use that as your out."

"If I really wanted to, though, you think I could settle down? Prove all my exes wrong?"

No chance in hell.

"Of course you could," I state with utmost confidence.

Do I like lying to my best friend? No. But Beckett hates being told he can't do something, and he especially hates when people try to tell him who he is as though they know him better than he knows himself. If I say he's incapable of commitment, he'll go find a girl who's completely wrong for him and do some stupid shit like elope to Vegas after one date. My lie isn't to avoid confrontation, it's to protect him from himself.

"You mean that?" he asks, watching the sideview mirror as he changes lanes.

"Yeah," I reassure him, eyes glued to the windshield. "When the right girl comes along, you won't think twice about settling down."

Chapter Three

THERE'S a torn piece of paper in my hand with words scribbled in a completely un-list-like fashion around the page.

> *Candles*
> *Matches*
> *Fancy food*
> *Music*
> *Gift*
> *Napkins*
> *Funyuns*

I snort at Beckett's odd idea for an anniversary dinner, mostly because half of the list doesn't need to be bought at the mall. "Becks, I'm pretty sure your parents have napkins and matches at home, so you can scratch those. And I know for a fact your mom has candles you can use—they're in the attic with your holiday decorations. I also have some you can borrow for the night if need be. Fancy food isn't exactly a meal idea, you have music on your phone that you can connect to the patio speakers, and... Funyuns? I—just why?"

He furrows his brow and leans over the paper. "Oh, those were for me. I got hungry while I was brainstorming."

I roll my eyes and scratch that off the list. "Then that pretty much leaves an anniversary gift and dinner. Are you planning to cook for them or order takeout?"

Beckett pops an Auntie Anne's cinnamon pretzel bite in his mouth, chewing as he considers his options. We're sitting on a bench beside the pretzel stand, and I'm balancing a Styrofoam cup of lemonade between my knees as I await his decision. Dozens of people mill around, filling the two-story structure with excited chatter and laughter, browsing store after store to take advantage of the end-of-summer sales.

"Since I'm not a good cook, takeout is the better option."

I squint, tapping his elbow as I piece together a plan. "That's not necessarily true. You used to make that one meal for your parents when you were a kid, didn't you?"

He eyes me doubtfully. "Parmesan Chicken Penne? Mac, I was, like, ten. I'm pretty sure my parents just humored me into thinking it tasted good. Besides, my dad always grilled the chicken, and I caught my mom seasoning the noodles once."

"Maybe, but they loved when you cooked for them. If

you want their anniversary to be special, you should do that."

He bites his lip thoughtfully, then angles his body toward me, bouncing his knee. "Only if you help me."

"When is it again?" I ask, as though I'd have any standing plans for the evening that weren't with Beckett anyway. Besides the local diner, where my schedule is incredibly flexible, I don't have much of a life.

"Saturday." He plops one last pretzel in his mouth, then hands me the small bucket to finish. I stick it between my legs beside the lemonade, then begin devouring the warm, fluffy cinnamon bites.

When I don't agree to help him right away, he pouts his lips and presses his hands together pleadingly. "Come on, tell me you'll help."

I *could* agree, we both know that I inevitably will, but it's more entertaining to watch him grovel.

I dust the cinnamon sugar off my hands before tossing the bucket in the garbage can beside me. "We'll see."

I rise from the bench and ruffle his hair with an indifferent shrug, wrapping my lips around the straw of my lemonade.

He stands as well, following me as I start toward the opposite end of the mall. We're on the second floor, which overlooks a small garden of fake plants in the center of the first, flanked by a Starbucks and jewelry kiosk.

"If you help me, I'll buy you a milkshake..." he teases,

picking up his pace to jog around me and walk backward.

"Bribes didn't work on me when I was ten. They don't work on me now."

"What if I said I'd drive you to The Milkshake Factory? Today." He continues walking backward, occasionally glancing over his shoulder to ensure he won't run into anything. "Come on, Mac, I know you can't resist a Jake's Shake."

I narrow my eyes and grind my teeth.

The man drives a hard bargain. The closest Milkshake Factory is an hour away in Pittsburgh, and I loathe driving in the city, so I rarely go. Besides, the Jake's Shake is the *ultimate* milkshake and the best dessert beverage ever crafted.

Thank you, Jake Guentzel.

I suck on my bottom lip to hide the smirk that threatens to break free, then attempt to change the subject, pointing at the jewelry kiosk visible below. "I have an idea for your parents' gift."

I veer to the left, around the railing overlooking the first floor, and lead Beckett to the escalator. When we reach the bottom, he follows me to the counter, speaking in a hushed voice. "I'm pretty sure my parents don't need new engagement rings. And I'm even more certain that I can't afford—" he leans over the counter, peering at the price tags through the protective glass "—literally any of these. I mean, a thousand dollars? Who spends that much on a tiny ring?"

I purse my lips, shaking my head in sympathy for the woman he ends up with. "Your poor future wife."

"What do you mean?" he asks, entranced by the glittering jewelry.

Pulling out my phone, I do a quick search. "According to Google, the average wedding ring costs close to six thousand dollars."

He gapes, blonde eyebrows screwing up on his forehead. "You're joking."

I tilt the screen toward him, which only further intensifies his disbelief. "You know my neighbor, Mrs. Portsend?"

He nods slowly.

"Well," I continue, knowing without a doubt that I'm about to shatter his naïveté. "She and her husband renewed their vows last year, and he bought her a twenty-five-thousand-dollar ring."

"Jesus," he utters. He leans against the counter, and the woman behind it shoots him a look of disapproval. "He spent that much on her *second* ring? Maybe I should rethink my stance on commitment. It might save me a lot of money one day."

I cough. "Commitment phobe."

He shoots me a dirty look and I crack a smile, moving a few inches to the left to show him a reasonably priced silver watch and matching bracelet. The bracelet has an anchor dangling from one of the chain links with a tiny diamond on its head. The watch is similar in design, but the anchor is printed on the clock's face as opposed to a charm. "I saw an ad for this in their summer collection a few weeks ago. I thought it would be a great gift for your parents since they met on a cruise, but I can find something else for them."

Beckett looks awestruck, but he's not staring at the jewelry. "You're actually incredible, you know that, don't you?"

I lift a shoulder, pressing my lips in a modest smile. "It's no big deal. I knew their anniversary was coming up."

"No, I'm serious." He takes my hand, searching my eyes intently. "This is exactly why I need your help with the dinner—and not just the cooking. I need you to help me plan it so the night isn't a total disaster." His lips crook to the side, and he laughs in spite of himself as he glances at the engagement rings before falling to one knee, enveloping my hand between his. "MacKenzie Roman, would you make me the happiest man alive and help plan a date for my parents' anniversary?"

Several people stop shopping to look our way, and I glance around uncomfortably, ducking my chin.

"Beckett, get up," I order with a tug on his hands. "People are staring."

"Nope," he says, determined. "Not until you agree to help me."

I heave a sigh. "Okay, I'll do it. Now will you just get up?"

"I'd prefer if you were a little more enthusiastic about it, to be honest."

"Get your ass up," I yank him to his feet. He chuckles lightly, pulling me to his side for a half hug. He holds me for a second before his voice rumbles in my ear. "You know, it's impolite not to kiss a man after you accept his proposal."

"Yeah, well, so is proposing without a ring," I counter, combatting the butterflies that swarm in my stomach. I pat his chest and casually step out of his grasp.

He winks, peering at me beneath long, blonde lashes. "And here I thought my love superseded materialistic values."

I snort, nudging his arm. "You're an idiot. Just buy the gift. I'm going to walk around while you check out."

While the cashier gift wraps both the watch and bracelet, I walk a few paces toward a nearby store with no intentions of shopping. I just need some breathing room.

"You ready?" He appears behind me and places his fingers on my elbow, a small white gift bag in hand.

I nod, and we head out into the stuffy summer day. Clouds coat the sky, leaving just enough room for the sun to slip through and make the air five degrees hotter.

There isn't an empty parking spot in sight as Beckett and I stride between row after row of cars until we reach mine. I'm glad he was paying attention to where we parked, because if it were up to me, we'd be wandering up and down every row, clicking the keys until we found my 2014 Wrangler.

A group of girls pass by as Beckett unlocks the car, and they smirk, openly scanning him from head to toe. I think I recognize some of them from Richlynd High, but they were a few grades younger than me, so I don't know them.

"Hey, Beckett," one of the girls, a short redhead with hips for days, says.

Beckett, however, knows everyone despite attending a different school than me. Our houses may only be a three-minute walking distance through the grass, but he technically lives over the hill, past Richlynd's district border.

He looks over his shoulder, lips quirking as he turns in the doorway. "Hey, Kim. How are you?"

"Better now," she says sweetly, slowing her stride so her friends are a few paces ahead. I swear, there isn't a girl in this town who doesn't want him. "I'm having a party later tonight. You should come."

"Yeah, maybe," he says noncommittally. "Who all's coming?"

"Just me and you," she says, eyeing him shamelessly as she backs toward her giggling friends. Her hips sway with every step, and I avoid glancing at Beckett to see if he's watching.

People like Kim make me glad we *didn't* go to the same school. Our relationship had the chance to develop without cliques or social obligations disrupting the natural order of our friendship. Who knows if we'd be as close if it didn't.

"You know her?" I ask casually. Beckett steps aside so I can get in the Jeep and slide across the bench seat.

He shrugs, turning the ignition. "Not really. Her brother goes to BC, so I've seen her around a bit."

I roll down the window, gripping the door panel. I want to ask how often "a bit" is but refrain. My bitterness is entirely unwarranted. I need to get my head on straight.

"So, I know I sort of blackmailed you into helping me, but would you still want to get milkshakes?" Beckett asks, snapping me out of my inexplicable bout of jealousy.

I blink twice. "What kind of question is that? Yes."

Then I glance at the dashboard to check the time. It's almost five.

"Unless you want to head home to get ready for Kim's, uh, *party*." I wince, hoping that didn't sound the way it did in my head.

I see his glance out of my peripheral, but I keep my eyes glued to the road ahead. "You're joking, right? Mac, I haven't seen you in months. You're the only woman getting my attention tonight."

"I know, but I don't want to hold you back. You don't have to hang out with me out of obligation. If you want to go—"

"I don't," he interrupts. "And I never hang out with you out of obligation. You're my best friend *by choice*. I thought you knew that."

I inhale deeply, closing my eyes and resting my head against the seat. "No, I do."

"Good," he says softly, seeming surprised by the prospect that he might want to spend time with other people. He has an entire life in Boston that I'm not part of, and even one outside of our friendship here in

Richlynd. He can't find it *that* strange that I'd assume I'm not the only person he wishes to spend time with.

We come to a stop, and I open my eyes, rolling my head to the side with a small smile when I feel him take my hand.

"You know, I really did miss you," he says meaningfully.

"I know." I squeeze his hand, eyelids heavy from the long day I've had. "You wouldn't be driving me across state lines to get a milkshake if you didn't—bribe or not."

He eases down on the gas when the light turns, one hand on the wheel and the other holding mine on my thigh. "To be fair, it's your gas money."

I roll my eyes.

As though he doesn't fill up my tank whenever we take mini road trips like this.

I close my eyes again, tightening my grip on his hand and allowing the car's vibrations to lull me into a translucent state. After a little while, only half awake, I say, "Hey, Becks?"

"Yeah?"

I swallow, allowing thoughts of heavenly hot fudge, cookies and cream, and brownies whipped into a divine concoction to cloud my reality. "Do me a favor and don't go back to Boston, would you?"

"'College dropout' *was* on my list of resolutions for this year," he says, mulling over the idea.

I force a laugh, though I don't find the prospect of him leaving again so soon funny at all.

The worst part about it being late July already is that

not only did we lose out on three months together, but he has to pack his things and head back to school for his senior year in less than three weeks. Then who knows where he'll end up after graduation. Because as much as I hate to think about it, I don't think his career endeavors will lead him home to Richlynd.

To me.

Chapter Four

As hard as I fought it, exhaustion overcame me during the drive into Pittsburgh.

The stilling of motion pulls me out of a deep sleep, and I groan, neck bent in the most uncomfortable position—cheek resting on my shoulder and the top of my head pressed against the window, which Beckett must have closed at some point.

I rub my eyes and crack my neck, pressing my fingers into the base of my skull for relief.

"How long was I out?" I grumble, immediately noticing the absence of Beckett's hand in mine.

He opens the car door and steps out, stretching his back before lending me a hand. "Around a half hour."

I groan again, allowing him to help me out of the Jeep. He locks the car while I comb my fingers through my hair and check my reflection in the window, then we cross the street and walk several blocks in silence while I wake up. When we reach our destination, Beckett steps up to the tall glass door and holds it open for me.

A few people sit at the two-person tables placed around the establishment, and I shiver as the cool air envelops me in a frigid cocoon.

"They need space heaters in here," I remark, wrapping my arms around myself as goose bumps rise on my skin.

Beckett agrees, rubbing his hands up and down his arms. He may be wearing long sleeves, but the material of his shirt is so thin it's almost sheer. "I'll be back. I think I left a jacket in your car last time we went out."

"'Kay, I'll get in line," I say, teeth chattering. Four people order ahead of me, then I step up to the counter that's decorated with an assortment of sweets.

"What can I get for you today?" a worker asks. He's young. Definitely in high school, judging by his boyish face and the way he fidgets when he speaks.

"I'll have two Jake's Shakes, please." I clutch the strap of my over-the-shoulder purse, sliding it to the front of my hip and digging around for my wallet.

"Anything else?" he asks, drumming his fingers on the edge of the cash register.

The temptation to add pretzel caramel bark to my order is more compelling than my will is strong, but I restrain myself. "No, that's all."

"Okay." He fiddles with a few buttons on the register. "That will be fourteen dollars—can I get a name for the order?"

"MacKenzie," I say, prepared to hand him my credit

card when Beckett reappears, pulling his wallet out of his pocket and handing the kid a few bills before I can stretch my arm over the counter.

"My treat," Beckett says.

Once the boy gives him his change, a warm hand touches my back, steering me toward a round table.

A light blue, zip-up hoodie is strung over Beckett's arm, and he holds it toward me. I wrap my fingers around the plush fabric, wanting nothing more than to zip myself up in its warmth and say *screw you* to my cute outfit.

"Aren't you cold?" I ask instead, noticing the raised hairs on his arm.

He lifts a careless shoulder and pushes the jacket into my grasp. "Nah, I'm fine."

"Are you sure? It's your jacket."

"It was in your car," he points out, as though that somehow implies I have claim over it.

I slide my arms through the sleeves and shiver, wrapping them around me to conserve heat. "Thanks."

A worker calls out my name and sets our drinks on the counter, so Beckett strides across the room to collect them as I sit at the table. The chairs are like pure ice against my bare thighs, and I suddenly consider sitting on Beckett's jacket instead of wearing it.

He sets my shake down in front of me and settles in the seat across from mine.

"I draw the line at giving you my pants," he says, gesturing to my legs, which are slightly elevated off the seat with the way my feet press on the ground, toes pointed.

My eyes trail his chest to where a button is clasped midway down his toned stomach, and I'm almost tempted to ask for his shirt instead. Although, for completely different reasons than needing additional clothing.

Averting my gaze, I wrap my lips around the straw and suck a clump of brownie and chocolate into my mouth. I close my eyes and savor the heavenly taste, momentarily forgetting everything else. "This is so good it should be illegal."

Beckett nods, deep blonde hair shaking with the movement. "It really should be. If we had one of these closer to home, I'd gain a hundred pounds."

I glance down at my thin thighs and waist, quirking my lips thoughtfully. "Eh, my hips could use the calories."

He drops his gaze to my waist, then clears his throat and picks up his drink for another sip.

After a few minutes, it's evident Beckett is cold even though he wouldn't admit it if I held a gun to his head. So, I stand, pick his drink up by the lid, and nod toward the door. "Come on, let's finish these outside. We can warm up on the walk to the car."

Heat smothers me the moment we step outside, and I shudder with delight.

The sun blares down in full force, and I have to squint to see the sidewalk ahead, holding my hand up to shield my face. My phone vibrates in my back pocket, and with renewed circulation in my fingertips, I twist over my shoulder and tip it back far enough to read the screen.

There's a text from one of my coworkers, Tayler Tate. We're not super close, but she's my only friend besides Beckett. We went to school together since sixth grade and lost touch a bit after graduation, but now we both work at The Corner diner in town, so we see a lot more of each other. Still, she typically only texts me when there's a good reason to.

Tay: *I can't believe you didn't tell me. I'd like to call myself psychic for predicting this years ago, but let's face it—anyone with eyes could see. Congrats! Hope you had a good vacation, too. See you soon.*

Puzzled, I read her message twice over in an attempt to make sense of it.

"Does this make any sense to you?" I ask, tilting the phone toward Beckett.

He leans in, lifting his hand to shade the screen as we slow our pace. When he's finished reading, his forehead creases. "Not at all. What do you think she's talking about?"

"No idea," I say, already knowing nothing interesting has happened in my life lately. "Maybe I'm finally getting a promotion? Or maybe my parents finally signed divorce papers? I mean, I'm sure all of our neighbors are surprised one of them hasn't turned up dead on the lawn with how much they scream at each other."

"You're such a cynic," he remarks between mouthfuls of milkshake.

I walk lazily, losing my balance and bumping arms with Beckett. "Says Mr. Commitment over here."

"Hey now, I'm a hopeless romantic," he teases, playfully waggling his eyebrows. "You just don't know that side of me."

"I'm pretty sure I know every side of you there is."

"Oh, do you now?" he challenges.

"Uh-huh. I know Happy Beckett, Sloppy Beckett, Irritated Beckett, Sad Beckett—"

"Are you really naming the Seven Dwarfs right now?" he asks dryly. He slurps the last of his milkshake and tosses it in a nearby trashcan before taking my empty cup and doing the same.

"Only Happy is one of the Seven Dwarfs. How do you not know that? See—I even know *Uneducated* Beckett."

"You don't know Boyfriend Beckett," he proclaims, and my cheeks instantly burn.

"I've met just about every girl you've ever dated. So, yeah, I know Boyfriend Beckett."

He opens his mouth to respond, but his attention is stolen by two girls strutting across the street. One of them, a stunning brunette with legs longer than the Mississippi, has zeroed in on Beckett.

My stomach ties itself into knots when I recognize her. I'd thought I escaped the hell that was high school when I graduated, but every now and then, I still cross paths with the demon spawn.

Feeling self-conscious in Beckett's oversized jacket, I

unzip it and slide my arms out—not because I'm too hot, but because, compared to the girls heading our way, with V-shaped slits on either side of their dresses and strappy red heels that make their calves look like a Greek goddess's, I feel like a hobo.

I glance up at Beckett, whose expression is a mixture of surprise and longing. Rolling my eyes, I fight the burn in my chest and slap his stomach with the back of my hand. "Put your tongue back in your mouth."

He spares me a disapproving glance, and I raise an eyebrow as if to ask, *am I wrong?*

"They're not worth your time, Becks," I warn when his eyes drift back to the brunette walking straight toward us.

He clears his throat. "You know them?"

I shake my head. "Not the blonde. I know the other one, though. She went to my high school. Her name was Lai—"

My sentence falls off and my eyes slam into Beckett's. Only now do I recognize that the surprise and longing I saw on his face moments ago was mixed with a hint of familiarity.

"You're joking," I mutter, biting my lip as she comes to a stop in front of us.

I know he said I wouldn't like his ex, but Lainey Cameron? *Seriously?* Has he lost brain cells while in college?

If the town's rumor mill is correct, she graduated college early and secured a job in the city, which explains why she's here now.

"You have some nerve, Beckett Harlow," she says, casting her eyes down at me like I'm a piece of trash on the street. Her pouty lips turndown when she concludes her assessment, and she shifts her attention back to Beckett. "We *just* broke up."

I can see her assumption as clear as day—we drove all the way out here together, I was wearing his jacket... This looks like a date, and in her eyes, I'm a downgrade.

Thankfully, her blatant disregard of me snaps Beckett out of his stupor. "Don't do that. You broke up with me, remember?"

She eyes me with disgust, licking her lips. Lainey is one of those pompous girls who could date three guys at once, all of whom know about the others and only want her more because of it.

She thinks she can get away with anything if she bats her eyelashes enough times. That might sound judgmental, but I've watched her and a dozen other girls do that very thing all my life. She may be on Beckett about commitment, but there isn't a bone in her body interested in settling down with one man. She's all about the chase, and guys are suckers for women they can't have.

"Don't worry, I remember," she says. "I just didn't think it would take you less than a week to move on."

"Mac isn't my girlfriend," Beckett says, and my stomach somersaults at the mere word on his lips in relation to me.

"Oh, I know." Lainey's nostrils flare. "It's all anyone

can talk about. And you know what the worst part is? Everyone warned me not to get involved with you."

"Look, I have no idea what you're talking about, but even if she were my girlfriend, this sounds like a problem of your judgment. Not mine."

"Maybe a little of yours," I mutter. He *did* go out with this chick, after all.

The corners of his lips quirk, but he flattens them almost immediately.

"Don't bullshit me, Harlow. I *know*."

"Well, that makes one of us." Beckett sighs, grabbing my wrist and tugging me away from her. "It was good to see you, Lainey."

"You're unbelievable," she snaps, crossing her arms as we move around her. "Mrs. Davenport *saw* you propose. And to think I even *considered* giving you another chance."

Beckett stops walking, and my lips part as I look up at him in surprise.

The mall.

I cup a hand over my mouth. That's what Tay must have been texting me about. Someone saw Beckett jokingly get down on one knee and misinterpreted the situation.

I can't ignore the satisfaction that overcomes me knowing Lainey thought her relationship ended because Beckett was afraid of commitment, and now here he is a week later, engaged to his best friend.

It's priceless.

Still, it's not true, and we can't have people thinking

we're getting married. Imagine if our parents caught wind of this and didn't even know we were dating.

Hold on—not dating.

What I mean is, our parents are going to think we're engaged and wonder when the hell we got together.

Swallowing my pride, I start to turn around. "Look, I think there's been a mix-up here because—"

"We don't have to explain a damn thing to you," Beckett finishes for me. Except, that's not at all where I was going with my sentence.

Next thing I know, he's pulling me across the street before I can utter another sound.

"What do you think you're doing?" I hiss, yanking my arm from his grasp once Lainey is out of sight. As we near my car, I steal the keys from his hand before he can dodge my question. "We can't have people thinking we're *engaged*."

"Why not?" he asks. His flippant attitude has my blood pressure rising.

"Why not? *Why not?*" I ask ridiculously, blinking like I'm trying to clear fog out of my eyes. "Because we're not together, is *why not!* How can you be so casual about this? What if our parents find out? Not to mention, no one who knows us would ever believe we're anything more than friends. We need to set the record straight."

Besides, if we tell Lainey now, I'm sure the rest of our town will know by the time we arrive home.

Beckett ignores me and makes a grab for the keys, but I close my fist around them and place it behind my back. Out of reach—or so I thought.

Beckett steps into my personal space, breath coating the side of my face as he reaches behind me, wraps his hand around my fist, and pries my fingers off the keys one by one.

He unlocks the car and pulls the door handle, but I'm still in the way, so he can't open it.

I clench his shirt sleeve in my fist, forcing him to look at me.

"What is—" I start to ask what his problem is, but then I notice the look on his face. The dip of his chin. The way he avoids meeting my eyes. "What's wrong?"

He shakes his head. "Nothing. I just think you're making a bigger deal out of this than it is."

"You mean, you *letting* someone think we're engaged?" I gape. "Beckett..."

"Come on, it's funny, right? Like you said, no one will believe we're together, so where's the harm? Besides, it wouldn't hurt my reputation for girls to think I'm capable of a serious relationship, even if it's just a rumor. And I'm sure you wouldn't mind if your mom stopped harping on you to get a boyfriend."

"I—" I blink rapidly, struggling to process his logic. "No. *No.*"

"What?" he asks innocently, trying to move me out of the way, but I won't budge.

"We are *not* going along with this, you dumbass." I jostle his arm, unable to comprehend how he thinks that's a good idea. He saw an opportunity to make himself look better in front of an ex and he took it—fine. But continuing to go along with the lie? Keeping up the ruse of an engagement when we've never so much as kissed? It would be impossible, not to mention, the sort of pressure that could inevitably ruin our friendship.

"I never said I wanted to. Don't put words in my mouth," he argues.

"I know how you think. You implied it in your own empathy-seeking way."

He cracks a smile at that, and the softening of his features eases the knot forming in my chest.

I touch his cheek and he looks away, chewing his lip. "You know we can't do that, right?"

He lifts his gaze with a dimpled grin. "Obviously. I just wanted to one-up Lainey. That's all."

I give a small shove. "Okay, but just to be crystal clear —we are, *under no circumstances,* faking an engagement."

"As you wish." He nods in agreement. "We can fill our parents in first thing when we get home so there's no confusion."

After we came to an agreement that *we are not going to let people think we're engaged to help his love life and get my mother off my back because it's morally wrong*—I made him repeat that sentence a few times just so it stuck—he drove me home. Then he walked back to his place even though I insisted I could drive myself home after dropping him off.

For some reason, despite the complete falsity of the situation, I'm nervous as I walk inside, afraid that my mother will be waiting for me with some sort of wedding planning scrapbook clutched to her chest.

If she hasn't heard anything about the engagement, then my job is easy—all I'll have to do is explain the misunderstanding.

However, if she heard about it while we were gone, then she had an hour, maybe longer, to stew in it, and I don't know how to break the truth to her.

The front door clicks quietly behind me, and I head toward the short hallway opposite the kitchen, which hides the stairwell leading up to my room.

I can't avoid this conversation, but I can put it off for a little if I avoid *her*.

Growing up under a mother who wants nothing more than her daughter to be in a relationship is stressful enough without having to tell her that, not only am I not engaged, but I also made up the mystery man I told her about at the airport. If I don't come clean, she'll automatically assume he's Beckett, and I can't have that.

I'm almost up the stairs, almost home-free, when a step groans under my weight.

"Mac, is that you?" Like a vulture, my mom rushes out of her office and into the kitchen.

"Yeah, I went to the mall and grabbed milkshakes with Beckett," I say casually, trying to keep my voice even. "Actually, the funniest thing happened—"

"Where is it?" she demands, reaching for—*oh God*—my left hand.

I lick my lips and back away, but only manage to trip on the next step up. I clutch the railing for balance, clearing my throat. "That's actually what I wanted to talk to you about. Beckett and I—"

"Oh, I knew it!" she interrupts, clapping her hands together with glee. "I just *knew* you were hiding something from me. And Beckett? You know, I always suspected the two of you were more than friends—of course, I could never ask you because you get so defensive about those kinds of things. No matter, my baby is getting married!"

"Actually, Mom, I'm not—"

"Your father always tells me to leave you alone about your love life, but I just knew it wasn't natural for you to be single for so long—not with how pretty you are. I mean, if it were any other girl in your position, I might think something was wrong with her that kept the boys away. But all along, it was because you were in love with Beckett Harlow! Oh, I knew this day would come— albeit, I thought it might come a little sooner. First thing tomorrow, we're going to start planning the wedding." She pulls me into her arms and squeezes me tight, practically sobbing into my hair. "Baby, I need to see the ring. I've been waiting your whole life for this moment."

I open my mouth, stunned by her ludicrous monologue.

So what if I prefer not to date? That doesn't mean there's something wrong with me. And it *doesn't* mean I'm in love with my best friend.

I take a breath, fully prepared to tell her the truth and condemn her for the judgment and high standards to which she holds me.

Just rip off the bandage. You're only twenty—her standards for your love life are ridiculous.

"I can't show you the ring, Mom."

She places her hands on her hips. "And why not? He proposed with a ring, didn't he? Don't tell me he proposed without a ring. I'll have to have a *long* talk with his mother. It's bad enough he didn't ask for your father's permission beforehand, but to—"

"Mom. *Stop.*" I squeeze my eyes shut.

"What is it? What's wrong?"

"The reason I can't show you the ring is because we're..." I hesitate, taking in her expression, which is painted with mixtures of worry and excitement.

Then, against my better judgment, I do something bad.

Something so wrong that the version of me lecturing Beckett an hour ago would travel through time to slap me back into reality if she knew.

Plastering on a fake smile, I shrug, dipping my hands into the front pockets of my shorts. "Because we're getting it resized."

Chapter Five

"YOU TOLD HER WHAT?" Beckett cackles hysterically on the other end of the line.

"Shut up, it's not funny," I scold him, disappointed in myself for being too spineless to tell my mom the truth. "She was being so... well, herself. I just couldn't take the single-shaming for one more second. I have to tell her the truth. I know I do. But it just felt so good to give her what she wanted for once."

I'm pathetic. I'm a grown woman, and I can't stomach saying no to my mom.

The silence on Beckett's end tells me he still thinks we should let this engagement rumor run its course.

"I told you we can't," I say sternly.

"I didn't say a word," he defends.

"I already had to convince her we want a long engagement so she wouldn't start calling venues first thing in the morning. What happens if she puts a down payment on something or surprises me with some big, expensive gift that I don't deserve?"

The thought of either of my parents spending a dime on this lie is just what I need to snap me back to reality.

Beckett sighs. "You know where I stand. You want your mom to stop nagging you about being single, well, even a temporary engagement would do that. Then, after our tragic breakup, she probably won't hound you about dating for at least a year.

"Have you met my mother?"

"Look, you said so yourself—it felt good to give her what she wants. Why not keep doing that for a little while longer?"

"Because it's *wrong*. And I highly doubt a broken engagement will make anyone think you're marriage material—not when you wouldn't be fulfilling the commitment. Why do you want this so bad?"

"Because it'll be fun," he says simply.

I grit my teeth. "Not good enough."

He sighs again and I roll over on my bed, putting him on speakerphone and staring at the ceiling. It's dark out now, and the only light in my room comes from my phone screen. "I want to prove to everyone that I'm not what they think. That I *can* commit to someone."

"But what if—"

"Three weeks. That's all I need. We'll tell everyone what you told your mom—we want to enjoy being engaged so we're not rushing into the wedding planning while I'm at school. If they want a date, then we'll give them one that's years away or something. We can break it off when I go back to Boston—blame distance or whatever. Please."

"I don't know…"

"Come on, Mac. You know it's going to be so fun screwing with everyone in town."

"I can't believe this." I sit up, pressing the heels of my palms into my eye sockets and slapping my cheeks a few times—a last-ditch effort to forget this stupid idea. It doesn't work. "I can't believe I'm agreeing. How did I let you talk me into this?"

He chuckles, but then the call disconnects.

I tap my phone, wondering what happened until I hear him call from below my balcony. "Because I'm your best friend, and I brought beer."

I get off my bed and push open the sliding door. The night is cooler than earlier, but the air is still sticky when I step outside in bare feet.

Beckett stares up at me with a cheeky grin, wearing a gray tank top that's cut past his ribs, leaving both his arms and sides exposed. I roll my eyes, craning my neck toward the dark sky.

"Are you boycotting front doors?" I ask, kneeling to reach my hand through the railing and grab the handle of the six-pack he lifts above his head. I work my hands up the slits until I've lifted it over the railing's ledge, then I set it on one of the folding chairs.

Beckett uses the grooves in a large oak tree to climb until he's even with the balcony, and I reach my arm out to help him.

"No, but I didn't want to run into your parents yet." He grunts, clasping my hand as he extends a leg over the railing, finding his footing in one of the slats. Then he swings his other leg over and plants his feet on the ground in front of me. He smirks with a wink, arm brushing mine as he leans past me to grab a beer. "Hey, fiancée."

"You do realize how stupid this is, right?" I ask, still unsure as to why I agreed in the first place. At the moment, I was annoyed with my mom, but hours have passed since then, and I still haven't managed to talk myself out of it.

He nudges me with his elbow, staring out at the grassy hillside as he twists the cap off a beer. "You've got to admit, MacKenzie Harlow has a nice ring to it."

I almost drop the beer he hands me.

MacKenzie Harlow.

Does he not realize how insane it drives me every time he makes some stupid, thoughtless remark like that?

I settle in a folding chair, taking a large gulp of my beverage before I trust myself enough to speak. "I don't see a way this ends well. If anyone finds out, we're going to look like terrible people."

"I can live with that. Anything else?" He sits down and rotates toward me so his shoulder rests against the back of his seat.

I pick at my fingernails. "Well, um, you know, in case anyone would ask... I told my mom you proposed with a two-carat, oval-cut diamond with a white gold garden setting."

I tighten my grip on the bottle, tapping a thumb as Beckett stares at me.

His eyes twinkle as he holds back his laughter. "And you just came up with that out of nowhere?"

"Yeah, well, I mean, she asked. So."

His teeth capture his lip, and he stands casually, setting his beer aside. Then he rushes into my room, sliding the door shut and turning the lock.

"What are you doing?" I call, twisting in my chair to watch as he lifts my bed skirt, then looks beneath my pillow.

Most of my drawers are half open with clothes spewing out of them, my nightstand is littered with pens and empty water bottles, and my bedding is strewn all over the floor.

Needless to say, I was not expecting company.

"Where is it?" He moves toward the left side of my room, away from my line of sight.

"Where's what?"

"When my cousin got married, she had a giant-ass scrapbook she'd compiled ideas in her whole life," he says, voice muffled. "There's no way you don't have one with a ring that specific."

"I don't," I lie, cringing as I picture the pink hatbox with princess crowns and wedding dress stickers plastered on the lid at the base of my closet. I'd forgotten all about it until now—I made it on a whim after I watched *Bride Wars* when I was thirteen. It's poorly hidden behind a photo album of senior year and—

Oh shit.

I rise from my chair and stumble to the door, jiggling the handle anxiously. "I'll show you; I swear. Just let me in."

I bang lightly on the glass, but I'm too late. Beckett emerges from my closet with a square whiteboard in one hand and my hatbox in the other.

Mortified, I turn away, cheeks burning red.

The lock clicks and Beckett slides the door open, clearing his throat. "And here I thought I knew everything about you."

"Shut up," I groan, moving past him into the bedroom. I grab the whiteboard from him and search for a tissue to erase it with. I can't even bring myself to *read* it because I'm sure it's ten times more embarrassing than I remember.

"Hey, I wasn't done reading," Beckett teases, laughter spilling over.

This is the most embarrassed I've been since Reggie Stevenson spilled his apple juice on my white pants in third grade and told everyone I peed myself.

I didn't think anything could ever top that moment, yet I find myself wishing to hear a chorus of *Pee-Pants MacKenzie* just to drown out my humiliation.

"Just pretend you never saw this. I'm begging you." I grab a clean sock when I can't find any tissues and push my thumb into the fabric, scrubbing the board.

"No way. How could I possibly forget you wanted your first kiss to be—" he appears behind me and leans over my shoulder, "'—at the top of the tallest hill of a roller coaster and/or in the rain?' Can you even ride a roller coaster in the rain?"

I elbow him in the ribs, and he chuckles, grabbing my upper arms when I try to move away from him.

"Lighten up, it's cute," he says, still laughing.

I toss the board aside when it's clear the marker won't come off. It's been there so long that I'm going to need more than a cotton sock to erase it.

Beckett sits on the edge of my bed, lifting the whiteboard into his lap so he can reread the list of everything young me wanted in a man.

"How old were you when you wrote this?" he asks, tapping the surface with a knuckle.

"Eight." I wriggle my toes, staring at them on the floor.

I can feel his disbelieving eyes on me.

I sigh, dropping down beside him. "Thirteen."

To his credit, he doesn't laugh at me this time. I scan the list, afraid of how bad the damage is since I don't remember everything I wrote.

It's worse than I thought.

MacKenzie's Future Hopes and Dreams: Romance Edition

1. Have my first kiss at the top of the tallest hill of a roller coaster and/or in the rain.

2. Have a summer fling with a lifeguard while on vacation.
3. Meet a prince who will whisk me away on a white horse (like the Taylor Swift song but happy).
4. Get married by twenty-three.
5. My husband will be my absolute best friend in the world.

I feel sick.

Beckett *read* this.

This.

There are some things even a best friend never needs to know—especially a male one.

"I have to say, I'm a little hurt by number five. You were really going to replace me with your dream man?"

I swat the back of his head, but he ducks out of reach. "Lucky for you, I haven't met him yet."

"For all intents and purposes, you *are* engaged to your best friend."

I give him a doubtful look. "I don't think a fake engagement is what thirteen-year-old me had in mind."

"Just think of it as a trial run for the real thing."

"But it's not. Not really."

The weight of his stare bores into my soul and sends shivers down my spine. Then he asks honestly, "Do you want to call it off?"

"No, I'm in," I say softly, and before I realize what I'm doing, my eyes drift to his lips.

I stand up quickly, praying against all odds that he didn't see that.

"I'm really tired. We can talk more tomorrow," I say, forcing a smile and wringing my hands together.

He blinks several times, standing slowly. "You're kicking me out?"

Yes.

"No, not at all, but I've had a long day, and it's almost eleven. I'll see you in the morning?"

"First thing," he says, though he doesn't look happy that our first night together in months is being cut short. Normally, we'd sit on the balcony until two a.m. bullshitting about everything and nothing at all. But as much as I want to spend time with him, my brain is on overdrive today and I need to think—something I can't seem to do when his eyes are on me.

This fake engagement is going to be a lot harder than I thought if I can't get this stir of feelings under control. Especially if we're put in a situation where we have to act couple-y. Things that Beckett doesn't think twice about get my heart pounding, and if I'm not careful, I'm the one who's going to get hurt.

"'Night, Mac," Beckett says, squeezing my arm before he steps onto the balcony and swings his leg over the side, dangling from the railing for a beat before he drops onto the grass below.

Scrunching my sleeves in my fists, I press them to my face and groan. Then I peer down at the stupid whiteboard again.

In the midst of my teenage years, consisting of an

unstable family and a lack of any other constants in my life, I didn't want to meet and marry a man who would *become* my best friend.

I wanted to end up with *my* best friend.

I'd thought I moved past that, but if today taught me anything, it's that one look from Beckett Harlow could raise those feelings from the dead.

Chapter Six

~~~

SHOUTING from downstairs drags me out of sleep the next morning, along with the scent of maple sausage coasting up the stairwell from the kitchen.

My stomach growls in response, knowing very well that if I want to eat, I'll have to walk through the crossfire. Rolling onto my side, I feel around the nightstand for my phone, then pull it as close to my face as I can with the cord still plugged into the wall.

I have three texts from Tay, one from Beckett, and a missed call from Ryan, who is probably calling to congratulate me on my engagement. He never calls for anything other than major life news, such as when I broke my arm as a kid, turned sixteen, or when he got engaged. He didn't even tell us Angela was pregnant until a month before their first baby was due. So, I have no doubt he's only reaching out to fulfill some empty, brotherly gesture now.

Ignoring his call, I open my messages and navigate to Beckett's contact, reading his text from fifty minutes ago.

Beckett: *Breakfast in an hour?*

Pursing my lips, I check the time. I have a shift at the diner in two hours, which gives us plenty of time to grab something to eat. I text him to be here in fifteen minutes, then move out of his conversation and scroll to Tay's name.

Tay: *Uhm... hello???*
Tay: *I've tried to be patient, but I need details.*
Tay: *Call. Me. MacKenzie.*

With a deep breath, I click call as I head into the bathroom to get ready for breakfast.

She answers on the second ring.

"If I weren't so happy for you, I'd be furious that I wasn't the first person you told—"

"We're not engaged," I blurt, unable to keep the secret in any longer and it hasn't been a full day.

There's silence on her end, and I take the opportunity to fill her in on most of what happened yesterday.

"Wow," she says, stunned. "Does it matter, though? You're in love with him either way."

"What?" My eyes bulge as I run a brush through my hair. I was careful not to tell her anything specific, especially not how every time Beckett touched me, I was dying to lean forward and kiss him. "That's ridiculous. I'm not in love with Beckett, he's my best friend."

"Hon, no two people who spend as much time together as you do are just friends. It's impossible."

"That's just not true," I argue, plugging in my flat iron. While it heats up, I apply a thin coat of mascara then throw on a black tube top and jean shorts. "How is it so easy for everyone to believe we're together when, as far as anyone knows, we've never dated?"

Lainey, my mom, Tay, whoever saw us at the mall— they all believed the rumors without hesitation.

"Because you've practically been dating for years. You do everything together, he gives you his shirt when you're cold, pays for everything, *and* drives your car." She laughs heartily, sounding almost sympathetic. "If anything, everyone is shocked it took you this long."

You're in love with him either way.

Tay's words ring in my ears the entire morning like the hook to a bad pop song.

If anything, everyone is shocked it took you this long.

She couldn't let me find peace in my state of denial. No. She had to push and prod at my defenses until I let a tiny ounce of the truth seep through.

Denial is safe. Protective. Nothing can hurt me in good ol' Denial Land because if I don't admit the truth, then my heart can't be shredded to pieces.

Besides, her implications would mean Beckett feels

the same way about me that *I do not feel about him,* and I can't bring myself to believe that's possible.

Sure, he has done chivalrous things for me since we were kids, but that's just who he is. If that's her only proof that we're in love with each other, then that would mean Beckett Harlow has been in love with me all our lives, and that isn't possible. Not when he's gone through more girls than I can count, especially recently.

And like a devil's advocate on my shoulder, I hear Tay's voice in my head.

Maybe the reason he's gone through so many girls is because they weren't you.

Regardless, I can't picture a world where he reciprocates my *non-feelings,* and I don't need those sorts of thoughts giving me false hope.

My feelings for him have come and gone as frequently as a common cold since I was a kid. They'll go away again.

I take a breath and pick up my turtle macchiato, sneaking a glance at Beckett while he eats. His eyes dart toward me on occasion, but I can't tell what he's thinking.

We chose a local café for breakfast, and far more people than I anticipated have congratulated us. It's like Tay predicted—they seem surprised it took us this long.

"I hear a celebration is in order." Carlyle, my next-door neighbor and head chef of the café, appears at our table. He removes his apron, wrinkled face bright with joy. "I knew you'd wind up here the moment I saw you chasing each other around MacKenzie's yard with the water hose as kids."

"I can't believe you remember that," I say, motioning for him to join us.

"Of course, I remember. Maggie and I used to watch the two of you from our front porch every afternoon. You were our main source of entertainment." Carlyle smiles fondly, and I feel a pang in my chest at the mention of Maggie. She passed away a few years ago, and since they never had kids, he was left alone. That's actually how he wound up working here—the owner needed a new chef, and Carlyle has quite the reputation from his yearly end-of-summer barbecue. He figured getting out of the house would be good for him. "Then winter would roll around, and every time it snowed, we would sit by the window and watch you kids sled down the hill. Maggie loved when your little heads would appear, bobbing closer to the top only to go down again. Do you remember the year your sled broke?"

I glance at Beckett, and he laughs at the memory, placing his hand overtop mine.

"I do," I muse, eyes on Beckett when I speak. "You convinced me we could still sled on garbage bags, and when that didn't work, we laid sideways and rolled down instead."

"Only because you refused to go inside," Beckett argues. "You had your puffy blue snowsuit on, and I'd had to force you to come outside to begin with, and then you wouldn't go in until you had fun." His thumb absently rubs my knuckles, and he drops his gaze before lifting it again. "You did have fun, though."

"I always did," I say thoughtfully.

With you.

The silent words hang between us, and I clear my throat, glancing at Carlyle, whom I almost forgot was sitting with us.

He stands, eyes twinkling as he looks between us. "I should get back to work, but it was wonderful seeing the two of you together."

"It was great to see you," Beckett says, and I agree.

The moment he's gone, I start to pull my hand out from under Beckett's, but before I can, he tightens his grip and slides his other hand beneath mine so it's sandwiched between them.

He shifts forward with a mischievous grin. "If we want people to think we're engaged, you can't be afraid to hold my hand."

"I'm not. I just..." I search for an excuse but come up empty. Though, I suppose *empty* would be better than what I actually say. "I just need both hands to... to cut my eggs."

I gesture toward the bowl of eggs in question—scrambled with mushrooms, peppers, onions, and feta cheese. None of which need "cut."

"Are you still freaked out about me finding your list?" he asks sincerely, lacing his fingers through mine and sending shivers down my spine. "You were a kid, Mac. And, sure, meeting a prince is a bit unattainable, but there's nothing wrong with dreaming big."

I pick up my fork and stab it into the fluffy eggs, then shove a hunk in my mouth and chew slowly so I can compose a response.

"No, I know that. This has nothing to do with the list."

"Then what?" he asks, entirely clueless.

I take another bite. "It's nothing. Want to take these coffees to go?"

He releases my hand, tipping back his chair with a short nod. "In other words, you want to go somewhere the whole town doesn't know us."

I open my mouth, feeling guilty. "No, not at all. I just... you're, like..."

I stumble over my explanation.

Don't say it.

Except, I can't hold it in, either. I've told Beckett almost every secret I've ever had, and I don't know how to stop now.

"You holding my hand kind of freaks me out."

He lets out a puff of air, lowering his voice. "Mac, I hold your hand all the time."

He rises from the table and grabs his coffee before exiting the café. I collect my thoughts and then follow, walking swiftly to keep up with him as he cuts through the park.

"I know," I exasperate, feeling like the worst friend in the world. "It just feels different now."

"Why? Because people *think* we're together? They always thought that. The only difference is now *you* know."

He stops behind a bench beside a pink dogwood tree, and I sit down, tipping my chin toward the sky.

"Becks, I'm sorry. I'm a little out of my comfort zone, and this is more pressure than I thought it would be."

He leans on the bench, resting his forearms beside my shoulder. "Because I held your hand."

It's not a question.

I turn to look at him, taking in his clasped hands, tight jawline, and pained blue eyes as they scan the sidewalk.

I shake my head, and I'm not sure what compels me to do it, but I brush my knuckles over his cheek. He inhales, dragging his eyes across the grass, up the bench, and to my face where they linger.

"You're right," I whisper, doing everything in my power not to tear my gaze from his. "I'm overthinking. Nothing is different."

"Exactly," he agrees, watching me so intently I forget to breathe. "We only have a few weeks of pretending, and then we can end the charade."

Right. *The charade.*

For him, this will all be over soon, but I'm certain that with or without this fake engagement, my friendship with Beckett will never be the same.

Chapter Seven

I WIPE a soapy rag across table after table until every crumb is gone, taking care to scrub the crusted-over sauces that dripped from customers' meals throughout the day. Then I use another rag to dry them, trying to keep my mind from wandering to Beckett. It's not unusual for him to stop by during one of my shifts, and every time the goddamn door opened today, I'd hoped it was him.

After the awkwardness this morning, everything went back to normal, and I think that's part of the problem. Everything is *too* normal, as though he's making an extra effort to prove nothing has changed.

I can't figure out why, after fifteen years of friendship, I suddenly want his friendly banter and good-humored punches to mean more.

"If you get that table any cleaner, you're going to sand off the design," Tay says from behind me, leaning against the soggy mop she's supposed to be cleaning the floors with. However, it's become evident she prefers harassing me to working. "Or are you imagining running your hands over Beckett's washboard abs?"

Rolling my eyes, I throw down the rag and wipe my wrist across my forehead to remove the hairs stuck to my sweat.

I told her the truth about me and Beckett in confidence, and the entire day, she made a big show of our engagement to every customer who came in.

"No. And Beckett doesn't have *washboard* abs."

"Ah-ha—" She jumps up, swinging the mop around so it points at me, splashing dirty water across the tables I just cleaned. "So, you *have* seen him shirtless."

"He used to chase me around half-naked with a hose when we were kids," I supply, unwilling to feed into her delusions.

One thing I determined today is that I need to sort out my feelings for Beckett on my own. And once I'm sure this isn't a whim... then I'll figure out what to do about them.

Tay puts down the mop, glossy lips pouting in dissatisfaction. Her black hair is pulled up into a tight bun, only a few curls falling loose around her face. "Come on, you can't have a body like that with a pudgy stomach, Mac."

A snort escapes me, and I purse my lips, returning to my cleaning. No, Beckett isn't a bodybuilder by any means, but the man has a *body*. He's lean, fit, and his stomach is damn toned.

"I see you smirking." She waves a finger around my

face. "I bet you're wishing he'd chase you around with that hose again, huh?"

"No, Tay," I say tiredly. "There's nothing between us besides a rumor. Let it go."

"You are absolutely no fun," she says grumpily, then claps her hands together and sits on yet *another* table I've already cleaned. "Okay, here's what we're going to do."

I squeeze my eyes shut, afraid she's going to devise a calculated plan to get Beckett to remove his shirt for her.

"We're going to get some people together tonight to celebrate your engagement. Force you two to spend some extra time together."

I don't bother telling her that regardless of where I am tonight, there's a ninety-nine percent chance Beckett will be there with me. Most likely my balcony. Drinking beer like every other night.

"Except we're not engaged," I hiss, looking around the empty restaurant. She and I are the only people scheduled to close tonight, so the rest of the staff has gone home already. Still, I'd rather be cautious than have this blow up in my face on day one.

She waves her hand. "Semantics. Don't you worry about silly details."

"It's not a silly detail if it's the entire purpose of the celebration," I argue, but her mind is already made up, and nothing I say will change it.

"Let's meet at that little bar on Tenth at nine-thirty and invite a few work friends. It'll be small, nothing crazy. Just think of it as a fun night with friends. It's the end of summer, we're young, you're—"

"Don't say engaged."

"—engaged. Live a little, Mac."

"I live," I argue, motioning for her to get off the table so I can rewash it. "I live *a lot.*"

She scrunches her nose but doesn't budge. "You do know breathing doesn't necessarily count in this instance, right?"

"Wow. Okay, then," I say, tossing the rag at her. "I'm going home. You can rewash this table and finish the last two yourself."

I exit the dining area and head down the hallway leading to the supply closet, where I deposit my apron in a bin labeled *dirty*, then grab my purse out of a cubby in the corner.

Tay sighs dramatically from the other room, but the sound doesn't signify defeat. It's the kind of sigh released when someone knows they're about to get exactly what they want. "That's alright. You know, I heard Kim Landry once had an affair with a married man—her friend's dad, of all people. I'm sure she'd have no qualms about kicking it with someone's fiancé." She pauses for a moment, letting her words sink in. "Hey, isn't she into Beckett? She was in here talking a mile a minute about him the other day. And you know, since he's not *really* engaged, he's technically free to do whatever he wants. Then maybe *she* can tell me just how ripped his abs are..."

"You're not funny, Tay," I grumble, closing the closet door and fighting the bout of jealousy that burns hot in my core despite her empty threat.

"Maybe I should message her. Tell her Beckett's been asking about her, too," she continues casually. "He might not be into her right now, but every guy has a breaking point. With the right amount of persistence, he'll give her a shot."

Slinging my purse over my shoulder, I head back in her direction.

"Nine-thirty, right?" I ask hoarsely, shoving through the front door so hard the bell rattles loudly, drowning out Tay's maniacal laughter.

The sky is a murky blue, clouds overcasting the sunset, and a few raindrops sprinkle in warning of the downpour to come.

I check the weather app on my phone to find there's a ninety percent chance of rain in three minutes. My house is only a ten-minute walk from the diner, so I usually use the opportunity to get some exercise, but I'll never make it home before it rains.

I start my trek down the sidewalk, crossing the street as lightning streaks across the sky.

Chewing my lip, I unlock my phone and click on Beckett's contact.

"What's up?" he answers on the second ring.

I scrunch my nose hopefully. "Any chance you could come save your fiancée from a rainstorm? I just left work."

I cross another street as the rain falls faster, picking up my pace at the base of the hill. It's a seven-minute walk straight uphill from here.

"That could be arranged," Beckett says.

Headlights blind me up ahead, and I shield my face as a truck slows, cutting across the double yellow lines to my side of the road.

Blinking in surprise, I end the call and jog around to the passenger side, yanking open the door and hopping inside.

"How'd you know I'd call?" I ask, floored. I drop my purse on the floor and give him a half hug in thanks, reveling in the cool interior of his truck. It's a nice change of pace from the humidity outside.

"I didn't." He hugs me back, speaking as I pull away. "I knew you got off at eight and saw it was going to rain. Depending on when you finished cleaning up, I figured I'd either meet you somewhere along the way or wait in the parking lot until you were done. Besides, you know I hate you walking home at night anyway."

I do know that. The closest we've ever come to an argument is after I started this job. He came home for the summer after his first year of college and couldn't believe I walked home in the dark, by myself, every night. I can't do it as often in the winter for obvious reasons, but when it's warmer out it's a nice way to decompress from whatever shitty shift I've just endured.

I had gone back and forth with him for days about it until he finally snapped. He said the thought of anything happening to me during the walk, especially while he was away at school, kept him up at night.

I never walked home in the dark again.

"Thanks for coming," I say, touched that he thought of me.

"No big deal," he responds, fingers pulsing around my thigh as I buckle my seatbelt.

He cuts back into the right lane and pulls up to the stop sign before doing a U-turn back up the hill.

I stare out the window as the interior lights flick off. "So, Tay wants to go out tonight to celebrate our engagement."

"I thought she knew the truth?"

"She doesn't care. She kind of blackmailed me into it, too," I admit, sparing him the details. "We're meeting at the bar on Tenth Street. Nelson's, I think."

Nelson's is the only bar in our neighborhood you can get into if you're under twenty-one. Every customer has to show their ID and is given a wristband to signal to the bartender whether they're of age. Most other bars won't take the risk and only admit customers over twenty-one after seven.

"You don't have to come if you don't want to," I add, just in case he's not up for it.

"Nah, I'll come. Besides, if Tay's there, it's guaranteed to be interesting."

"How so?" I ask.

Beckett smirks, tipping his head back on the headrest.

"Is that jealousy I detect in your voice?" he teases, taking his eyes off the road to glance at me.

I puff out my lips, shaking my head in denial. "Nope. You're just not allowed to find other girls interesting."

"Is that so?"

"Mmhmm," I hum. "Only me."

"You know, I think I can live with that," he says, shifting the car into park when we reach my driveway.

I smirk, unbuckling my seatbelt. "Yeah?"

"Yeah. You're certainly interesting enough to account for three other people."

"Shut up." I swat his arm. He rests his hand on the steering wheel, thumb tapping as he laughs.

Silence falls over the car as we listen to the rain pounding on the windshield. If I get out now, I'll have to wash my hair before we go out, and then we'll definitely be late.

"Since Nelson's only has parallel parking, want to drive over to my place and we'll take your car since it's smaller?"

"Sure." I nod. I hate the part of me that wants his offer to be, not practical, but an excuse to spend more time alone with me before we go.

Which is a ridiculous thought to have.

But then...

"Did you eat yet?"

"No," I say. I often grab a burger after my shift because employees get free meals, but since I closed tonight, I didn't want to make any of the cooks stay longer than necessary.

"Me neither," he says, blue eyes scanning my face. "Want to get ready at my place and I'll order a pizza?"

My stomach growls in response. "Yeah, sounds good. I just have to throw makeup and clothes in a bag, then I'll drive back over."

"Okay, what do you want? Pepperoni and—"

"Banana peppers?" we say at the same time.

"Obviously." I smile, opening the door when the rain slows. "See you in a few."

"Bye, fiancée," Beckett calls before I close the door. I roll my eyes and shoot him the finger as I walk between my parents' cars, stopping at mine to throw my purse inside for later.

He doesn't drive away until he knows I'm in the house, and I wave through the window as he backs down the driveway.

Steam floats up from my flat iron as I close the prongs around a long strand of blonde hair. Beckett is on his bed with a perfect view of the bathroom mirror, and he watches me through it with his brow pinched and a piece of pizza halfway to his mouth.

Everything about his apartment is entirely *Beckett,* with hardwood floors, a La-Z-Boy chair, and a flatscreen TV that stretches across the wall in the alcove by his bed.

"This again?" I ask, already knowing what has him perplexed.

He takes a large bite of pizza and leans on his forearm. "It's the same concept as ironing clothes."

I snort. "When have *you* ironed clothes?"

"I see your point." He bites his inner cheek. "You sure you don't want more pizza?"

"If I eat any more, I'll feel like a walrus in these jeans

all night," I say, gesturing to the six-button skinny jeans hugging my hips like a glove.

His eyes travel the length of my body, then lock with mine through the mirror. He clears his throat and shifts onto his back, crossing his ankles. I'm not sure if he meant for me to catch him staring, but he says in a casual tone, "I'm pretty sure you have nothing to worry about."

I pretend to check my phone to avoid responding and notice a text from Tay. "Tay's at the bar already with two of our coworkers, Hannah and Elle."

I'm not close with either girl, but at least they can pose as a buffer between the two of us and Tay.

"Gabe and Tyler texted that they're coming—I'm not sure how they know about tonight, but I'm assuming Tay got ahold of them somehow."

"Doesn't surprise me," I remark, unplugging my flat iron and brushing my hair one last time.

Gabe and Tyler went to Beckett's high school, and from the few times I've met them, they seem like pretty decent guys. Not to mention, they're insanely attractive, which is likely why Tay made sure to have a way to contact them.

"You know, I was thinking..." Beckett starts, sitting up when I flick off the bathroom light.

"Nothing good ever comes of that," I remark, putting my stuff in the bag I brought and heading over to his bed. I hoist myself onto the tall structure, open the pizza box, and take another slice—walrus gut be damned.

"If we want people to believe we're a couple in public,

we should probably act that way in private, too. You know, for practice and stuff. That way we don't have a repeat of this morning."

"Practice?" I echo, chewing slowly. Beckett slides off the mattress and takes the pizza box with him, making his way to the fridge. "Like... holding hands for fun...?"

I finish the slice of pizza while he puts the leftovers away, then brush off my hands and follow him to the door. It opens to a flight of stairs that descend to a single garage, but I hesitate, turning to look at him.

The white dress shirt he wears hugs his biceps, rippling where the sleeves are rolled halfway up his forearms, accentuating his build.

I'd be lying if I said my eyes don't linger for a second too long.

His hand rests on the door, and his tongue darts across his lips as they turn up suggestively. "Or we could practice making out."

I huff, rolling my eyes at his overused joke. "You need a new punchline."

He's on my heels as I jog down the stairs, and when we reach the bottom, he leans past me to turn off the light switch, closer than necessary. "Who says it's ever been a punchline?"

His teasing tone damn near sends me to an early grave, but he turns away without looking at me.

Outside, he pulls a set of keys out of his pocket to lock the door. "I'm just saying, what if someone makes us prove we're together or something? I don't know about you, but I don't want our first kiss to be sloppy and in public with a bunch of people watching."

Our first kiss?

"You say that like it's inevitable."

Personal feelings aside—and by personal feelings, I mean the blissful terror that strikes me at the thought of kissing him—he has a point. Though, I doubt anyone would force us to prove we're in love with some public display of affection. Not to mention, kissing would severely cross the line considering this entire arrangement is fake.

Beckett might be cool with playing it off like it's nothing, but I don't think I could ever go back to the way things were if he kissed me. I'm struggling enough as it is.

"It's just a thought," he says as he opens the door to my Jeep.

I blink rapidly, chewing on my lip as I take his hand and step onto the running board. "I'll think about it."

I'll do what now?

It's as though my lips are conspiring against me.

I did *not* mean to say that.

Subconsciously, I consider laying one on him every time he makes a stupid joke about kissing me just to shut him up, but until this week, I never thought I would want to so badly.

Muddying the waters unnecessarily, for practice of all things, would just make things more complicated in the long run. Especially if we want to preserve some semblance of friendship when we "break off" our engagement in a few weeks. It's going to be difficult enough convincing everyone that there isn't residual tension after the breakup since we'll still be friends. I don't need to be fighting real feelings on the inside.

Now, if, say, he wanted to kiss me for a reason other than practice...

Maybe I'd reconsider my stance.

Chapter Eight

GABE AND TYLER arrive at the bar shortly after Beckett and I show up, and despite my concern that tonight might be awkward, given none of us know each other all that well, it hasn't been half bad so far.

Elle and Hannah are perched on barstools beside me, absorbed in a conversation about an obnoxious customer from yesterday who left a penny tip. Tay has been pressed up against Beckett's friends all night, and since I'm not close with anyone besides her and Beckett, I just listen in on both conversations.

Tay's cousin is working the bar, and she all but insinuated he wouldn't be opposed to giving us real drinks if we say we're with her. Which means, it's likely more than pomegranate juice eliciting her flirtations.

"He was one of those people who order well-done steak and then send it back because it's 'too dry,'" Elle says, wispy bangs styled on her forehead.

Hannah nods in agreement, and her long brown hair

shimmies with the movement. "If I could work anywhere else I would, but no one else outside my hometown is hiring."

"You don't live in Richlynd?" I ask, joining the conversation.

"No, I'm twenty minutes away from here." Hannah swivels on her stool so she's facing me. "I live in the middle of nowhere in a town so barren we don't even have a grocery store. It's impossible to find work unless I drive out this way. When I was a kid, I used to beg my parents to move here."

I wrinkle my nose. "It's not all it's cracked up to be. We're large enough to have two school districts but small enough that everyone knows everyone. Trust me, you were better off where you were."

Hannah purses her lips. "Oh, I can't imagine. I have a few cousins who live nearby, so I've heard stories. I'm sure all of the parents' drama was sent to school with the kids."

"Pretty much. You could only be friends with kids whose parents liked your parents," I explain with an eye roll. "My folks weren't like that, but mostly everyone else's were."

"Besides mine," Tay intervenes, moving between me and Hannah to set her cup on the bar. She taps it twice, and her cousin tops her off.

"You lived with your grandma, didn't you?" Elle asks, stirring her drink.

"Yeah. My dad was a deadbeat, and my mom wasn't equipped to be a parent, so she dropped me at my Nana's house and never looked back." Tay picks up her new drink, giving us her life story as though describing what she ate for breakfast. "It's a good thing Mac never had a life, or I wouldn't have landed a job after Nana died."

Tay's grandma passed away a month before we graduated high school, and her death is what ultimately reconnected the two of us. Tay had needed to make money to keep the lights on, and I put in a good word for her at the diner. And although that was a good thing for her, it somehow comes off as a dig into my social life.

If I didn't work as hard as I did, our boss wouldn't have given my request a second thought.

"You can't blame the parental gossip mill for your lack of friends," she continues blandly, and I wonder if she's trying to turn the conversation away from herself. Tay's eyes trail over Beckett, and she shoots me a suggestive look. "You've always been all work and no play."

"That's not true," I murmur, growing uncomfortable by her change in tone.

"Isn't it?" she presses, wrapping her lips around two cocktail straws.

Hannah and Elle exchange a look, sensing the subtle tension between us.

Tay's acting like she invited me out all the time and I refused her. We hardly saw each other back then, and that was fine with me. She had a lot of abandonment issues to work through, and her ways of coping weren't necessarily healthy.

As for her insinuation that I never put myself out

there with Beckett—she's right. But I never wanted to be with him badly enough to risk ruining our friendship. I've always been happy with the way things are, and there's nothing wrong with that.

Not everything we pine for in life is meant to be pursued.

"Just because I work hard doesn't mean my life is devoid of excitement."

"Huh, I must be thinking of a different MacKenzie Roman, then," she says, teeth clamping down on her bottom lip. "Because she was a real dud."

Tay downs her new drink and sets the cup back on the counter, rising to her toes to get her cousin's attention.

"I think you've had enough, Tay," I say, though I know that comment won't get me anywhere.

"*Thank you,*" she says, eyes widening as she picks up a straw and sticks it between her teeth. "For proving my damn point."

Hannah clears her throat, glancing at Elle again. "I don't know, Tay. Maybe she's right. You should slow down a bit."

"*I* know what you need," she says eagerly, completely ignoring Hannah. Then she turns around and disappears into the crowd of moving bodies on the dance floor. Her head bobs up when she reaches the DJ, rising onto her toes to yell in his ear.

Tay has always been forward—the perfect balance of sweet and vivacious. Most people love how her brutal honesty is delivered in the undertones. In reality, she's pushy, which I had forgotten until tonight. She all but strong-armed me into coming to what isn't much of a celebration at all. Suddenly, I wonder if she just wanted an excuse to go out, flirt, and drink since her cousin was willing to funnel her booze.

I glance over my shoulder to find Beckett watching me. He's a few feet away, nodding along to a conversation, but my face must indicate something's wrong because his demeanor changes subtly. He starts to move toward me, but then Tay returns, looking pleased with herself.

I tear my gaze from Beckett when she leans in close, fruity perfume tickling my nose as she clutches my forearms, whispering so only I can hear. "I requested a special song for you guys."

"Tay, come on," I beg, pinning her with a serious look. "Just because you think there's more here doesn't mean you should force it on us."

"*Wrong*." She tosses her short, curly hair over a shoulder. "That's exactly what I should do. If I leave it up to the two of you, you're going to end up forty, single, and still hanging out on the balcony of your parents' house."

I clamp down on my tongue, increasingly frustrated by her persistence. I understand that she's trying to help in her own way, but the last thing I need is for her to complicate things.

"Tay, you need to stop."

Her lashes flutter. "You'll thank me one day."

"That's not the point," I say louder than I intended, but she isn't fazed by my anger.

This entire night was a mistake.

"Is everything okay?" Hannah asks tentatively. She and Elle are both watching us, but with the music and chatter all around, they couldn't hear a word we said.

Tay smiles brightly, bouncing on her heels. "Everything's perfect. Mac was just telling me that she wants to learn how to loosen up a bit."

"Tay, that's enough." I take a breath, glancing at Hannah and Elle. "Can one of you make sure she doesn't drive home tonight?"

Tay grabs my arm, looking hurt. "You're leaving?"

"I am," I say, shaking her off and walking toward Beckett, who looks like he's having a great time. Maybe I'll tell him I want to leave and offer to pick him up when he's ready.

Hell, I'd sit in the car alone for the next two hours just to get out of here.

As I reach him, the R&B song that's playing comes to an end, and the following song is noticeably slower than the usual club mixes, transitioning into a sort of blues-inflected ballad that I recognize almost immediately.

"I've been told we have a future bride and groom in the audience tonight," the DJ says over a microphone, and several people in the crowd holler.

Here I was an hour ago, thinking the fake engagement was my biggest problem. Little did I know it'd be the threat of jail time.

Because I truly might murder Tayler Tate tonight.

"Where are you crazy kids?" he asks, searching the crowd.

Tay comes up behind me and tugs on my arm.

"I don't want to dance," I express, but she shoves me toward Beckett and lurches him to his feet.

"They're over here!" she yells, and every eye in the vicinity is on us. "Mac and Beckett."

"Well, Mac and Beckett, this song goes out to you. I wish you the best in your life together. Now, get out on that dance floor."

The song turns up, and several couples gravitate together and begin swaying to the melody.

"I said I don't want to dance," I hiss at Tay, but then Beckett is in front of me. He raises an eyebrow, a lazy grin slung across his lips that deepens the dimples in the corners of his mouth.

"You don't?"

"I—wait, you do?" I counter, suddenly feeling winded.

He heaves a sigh, but I can't decipher his mystified expression. Lightly touching my elbow, he slides his fingers down my arm until they curl around mine, then he tugs me toward him, teeth capturing his bottom lip with a smile as he casually moves backward. He drags me to the center of the floor, deep enough in the crowd to be somewhat shielded from our friends' prying eyes.

Beckett comes to a stop but continues to draw me closer until there's hardly any space between us. He lifts the hand still holding mine and deposits it on his shoulder. Then he reaches for my other hand and follows the same motion before placing his on my waist, applying just enough pressure to make me sway with him.

"Clever song," he remarks as 'Rumor' by Lee Brice plays over the speakers.

"Tay sure is clever," I say quietly, tongue caught in my throat. I find that once I meet his gaze, I can't look away.

"You seemed upset before," he says quietly. "What happened?"

"It doesn't matter now," I say, mostly because I can't remember. His proximity is suffocating, and all I can think about is our conversation at his apartment.

He bites his lip and tears his eyes from mine for a moment. "You know, I should have told you earlier, but you look..."

"Like a girl for once?" I supply humorously. I'm oddly uncomfortable in my skin, made even more so by the hand that slides up my hip and around my back, making it so I'm flush against him.

Like a girl for once?

Since when do I *not* look like a girl?

He cracks that same bewildered smile as before, watching me in a way that I can't quite interpret. "Trust me, I've never for a second forgotten you're a girl..."

His voice trails off and his eyelids lower with his gaze. He leans forward slightly, so close that his nose brushes my cheekbone. "I told you we should have practiced making out. If we kissed right now, I bet Tay would faint and we could go home."

A short breath expels from my lips, and I close my eyes to mask my disappointment.

He's watching *them*.

That's all this is. He's putting on a show. Keeping up the ruse.

And yet...

"You want to leave?" I ask, and the voice that comes out is flirty and completely not my own. Not a voice I use when talking to Beckett. Ever.

If it's even possible, he moves closer and rests his forehead against mine, faint breaths coating my upper lip. "No. I like being right here."

My throat bobs and goose bumps slither across my arms. My fingers find the hair at the nape of his neck, and I take a long breath, realizing I've been holding it since he pulled me in.

My eyes flutter closed, and my next words come out raspy. "Me too."

"Yeah?" He sounds oddly surprised, and I'm tempted to open my eyes, but decide against it. I'm always trying to find hidden meanings behind his eyes, in the quirk of his lips, but maybe I've been searching for the truth in all the wrong places. Maybe it can't be found in his expression, but instead in his tone of voice. His gestures. The way his hands absently slide across my back and trace the straps of my black halter top where my skin is exposed.

I can't comprehend how Beckett could feel anything more for me than friendship, and yet, friends don't dance like this.

For the first time since I've known him, I see a glimmer of truth.

We're not friends.

The song ends, but neither of us attempts to put distance between us. We continue to sway when the next song begins, and at a certain point, I can't stand the space beneath where our foreheads touch.

Instead of kissing him like I desperately want to, I slide my arms down his shoulders and around his waist, clasping my wrists behind him and resting my cheek on his chest. The bridge of my nose fits perfectly against his throat, where the top button of his shirt sits, unbuttoned. His chest rises and he holds me close, continuing to guide our bodies in a slow, swaying motion.

I have no idea what song is playing—I can't hear it over the blood rushing to my ears—but I have a feeling it could be 'Shots' by Lil Jon and I wouldn't notice.

"They're turning the lights on," Beckett says, and his chest vibrates against me.

I lift my head deliriously, and he loosens his grip.

My adrenaline is pumping madly, and there's a slight tremble in my hands when I release his waist.

The overhead lights are on, and the dance floor is slowly breaking up as the DJ finishes the final song of the night.

When I glance at the bar, I only see Hannah, leaning with her back pressed against the counter as she yawns into her fist.

"I'm going to run to the bathroom before we leave," Beckett says, and in the next second, he's halfway across the room.

I feel like I'm moving through quicksand as I place

one unsteady foot in front of the other until I'm beside Hannah.

"Where is everyone?" I ask, flushed and nervous.

"Tay was pretty drunk, so Elle and Ty took her home," she says, checking the time as she yawns again. "I didn't want to bother you guys, so I stayed behind to make sure we didn't disappear on you."

"Oh," I say, rubbing my arms and feeling guilty. "You didn't have to do that. You have my number from work, you could have texted that you left."

Hannah glances toward the bathroom, where Gabe emerges with Beckett not far behind him.

So, she *isn't* the only one who stayed.

"That's okay. I wasn't ready to leave yet."

"Gabe seems nice," I say, and she nods, tucking a strand of brown hair behind her ear.

"Yeah, he's sweet," she says, glancing at the guys before lowering her voice. "Look, I wasn't going to say anything, but Tay told me about your, uh, *arrangement*. And if she told me…"

"She'll probably tell Elle and Ty on the way home." I pinch the bridge of my nose, trying not to let Tay's actions ruin an otherwise good night. "You probably think we're terrible people, huh?"

Hannah waves her hand dismissively. "Not at all. You and Beckett are really good together, though. I hope it works out."

My stomach twists into knots. "Thanks."

When the guys reach us, she changes the subject like nothing happened, looking between me and

Beckett. "Do you guys need a ride home? I'm dropping Gabe off."

Beckett shakes his head. "We brought Mac's car, but thanks, Hannah."

"No problem," she says, smiling, but my attention is still on Beckett. He hasn't looked at me once since we stopped dancing, and he made a bogus excuse for the bathroom when it'll take us less than five minutes to drive home.

What if dancing like that makes him feel awkward around me now? What if he wanted to stop dancing but then I latched onto him like a parasite?

I shut my eyes and try to suppress my nerves.

Don't do this to yourself.

Beckett initiated the dance. He physically put *my* arms around him. He rested *his* forehead against mine.

Whatever happened tonight, I refuse to let fear convince me it was all one-sided. I can't do that to myself. I won't.

"Drive safe," Hannah says, and I'm pretty sure the three of them were still talking and I missed every word.

Before she can follow Gabe out the door, I touch her arm.

"In case you're looking to prolong your night, the park has a gorgeous outlook for stargazing. Beckett told me once that Gabe loves astronomy. And *Game of Thrones.*"

Hannah smiles, seeming impressed.

"You're officially my new wing-woman. Thank you." She then turns to catch up with Gabe and says, "Have you ever been to the park at night? I hear the stars are beautiful."

I'm pretty sure I witness him falling in love right there in the doorway.

We split off on the sidewalk, with Hannah and Gabe walking to the left, flirting so heavily that I feel a slight pang of longing since Beckett and I haven't spoken a word.

He removes the keys from his pocket and unlocks the car, walking slightly ahead of me to get the door.

I mumble my thanks and slide to the passenger side, buckling my seatbelt and gripping it like a lifeline.

This. This is exactly what I was afraid of. We got too close tonight and now he's pulling away.

The sudden urge to cry overwhelms me, but I force it down.

"You can stop at your place, and I'll drive myself home," I say as we near the hill.

"No, I'll take you home. I can walk to my place."

So, he does speak.

I moisten my lips. "You sure?"

"Yeah," he says, even though it would make more sense to drive to his house since it's closer.

Desperate to break the silence, I lean forward to turn up the radio, and I nearly break the knob rushing to shut it off when I hear what song is playing.

'Rumor' by Lee Brice.

My first instinct is to blame Tay for this. She has probably been drunk dialing the station all night to convince them to play it *right* when we left the bar. But even she couldn't have timed this so perfectly.

We're nearing my house when Beckett jerks the car into a grass field along the side of the road. There aren't any residences on this stretch, just grassy plains that stretch across several acres.

"This is ridiculous." His hand grips the steering wheel tightly, and he grits his teeth. After a moment passes, he decidedly turns the radio back up and opens his door, leaving it ajar as he walks around the front of the vehicle, spreading his arms wide. "Dance with me."

I roll my ankles around, tapping my heels on the floor mat. "Here? This is technically trespassing."

"It's a three-minute song," he yells over the music.

I scoot toward the driver's side, and he comes to help me out of the car before tugging me around the front, where the headlights bathe us in light. The song echoes around us, seeping out of the open car door and filling the air with electricity.

He spins me without warning, then pulls me close and dips me low to the ground.

I can't help myself; despite the nervous tension swimming between us, I laugh. "I didn't know you could dance like that."

He draws me nearer, shrugging modestly. "Just the basics."

Then he proceeds to extend his arm, sending me away before spinning me back toward him again. I twirl faster now that I'm expecting it, so fast that I can't stop myself before I collide with his chest.

"This is the extent of my knowledge," he says with a smile, completely aware of how goddamn sexy he is.

"So, now I know Dancer Beckett, huh?" I tease, enjoying the change of pace. This dance, unlike the last one we shared, is lighthearted. Fun. Proof that one moment can't ruin the sturdy foundation we've built over the years.

Beckett keeps a tight hold on my hand as he dances us in circles, resting his other arm lazily on my waist. "I'm almost certain you know every side of me there is."

I arch my brows playfully. "You're secretly taking dance classes in Boston, aren't you?"

He dips me again, bringing me up slower this time. His face is so close to mine that I'm afraid to breathe. "You caught me."

"I knew it," I say weakly, but as the song fades and sounds of the night creep through the silence, so does reality. Crickets sing, and the trees bustle in the warm evening breeze, but the moment is over.

"We should head home," he says, and I nod reluctantly, afraid of what tomorrow will hold for us.

My heart is heavy as I get back in the Jeep, gaze stuck on Beckett's every movement.

I can't stop wondering if tonight somehow altered our friendship forever. And if we did... is that really the travesty I've always imagined it would be?

Chapter Nine

THE WINDOWS ARE DOWN as I drive across town with the radio turned up as loud as it goes, thumb tapping the steering wheel to the base of a country song.

When I woke up this morning, everything felt different. I slept a total of four hours off and on because I couldn't slow my pulse long enough to relax. The whole time, all I kept thinking was *I needed that*. I needed to know I wasn't alone in feeling this way, and from the way Beckett held me, I think he did, too.

Except, I have no idea what it means for us or where to go from here. I've checked my phone obsessively since I woke up, but he hasn't texted me about breakfast. Sometimes when we've been up late or he has a busy day ahead we don't go, but still, today of all days is not the time to change our routine.

Instead, I woke up to a text from Hannah, asking if I wanted to grab brunch at a restaurant outside of town.

Since I haven't heard from Beckett and only have to work a short afternoon shift today, I agreed.

She seemed really nice, and I'm eager to find out how her night went after she and Gabe left Nelson's.

Besides, I desperately need something to take my mind off of Beckett.

After he drove to my house last night, he tossed me the keys, said goodnight, and headed home. He didn't even text me when he got home like usual. And if we're talking *like usual,* he normally would have begged me to keep the night going, but he didn't.

I twist the volume knob as I turn into the parking lot, spotting Hannah at a table outside the restaurant's large glass window.

I hop out of my car, and she looks up when the horn beeps, smiling and setting her phone aside when she sees me.

Her hair drapes over her shoulders, caramel highlights seeming brighter in the early morning sun. She's wearing a pair of jean shorts and a loose, deep red tank top with a black checkered pattern across it. "Thanks for coming."

"Thanks for asking." I smile, clutching my purse strap as I sit at the table and cross my legs. I've never been much of a girl's girl, so I feel out of my element with Hannah. She seems like a genuine person, though, which eases some of my anxiety. "Did you and Gabe have fun at the park?"

She tucks her hair behind her ears with a bashful smile. "Yeah, it was great. We talked all night about, like, everything, and then suddenly the sun was rising, and we were still lying in the grass talking."

"Now I know why you suggested brunch instead of breakfast," I joke, noticing the dark circles under her eyes.

She snorts, pressing her palms to her cheekbones with a bemused laugh. "Yeah, well, I need coffee if I'm going to make it until the barbecue tonight. Gabe said it's a tradition the whole town does every year?"

"That's tonight?" I gape, having completely forgotten. It's always on the last day of July, no matter when in the week it falls. Just about every business in town shuts down, and if they don't, they know to expect a lot of fake sick calls. It's the one day a year that you can skip work and not get fired for it.

Hannah nods. "Yeah, Gabe texted me a picture of them setting up in someone's backyard. Are you going?"

I run a hand through my hair. "Maybe. I'm not sure yet."

This is the one event I look forward to every single summer, but the last thing I want is to deal with everyone asking about the engagement.

"Gabe and I can play interference between you and nosy townsfolk if that's what you're worried about," she offers easily.

"What I really need is someone to tranquilize Tay," I remark, and Hannah throws her head back laughing.

"You joke, but my great-uncle works for animal control. We could make that happen."

A waitress stops at our table to leave a basket of steaming biscuits and a few packets of butter.

"Help yourself," Hannah says, immediately reaching for a biscuit and tearing off a hunk. "This is my first meal of the day, so I wanted something with substance. Also, I called Elle a little while ago—she didn't say anything about you and Beckett, so I don't think Tay said anything to her or Tyler."

"Thanks, I appreciate that. This whole thing is just... so stupid," I say, grabbing a packet of butter. I peel off the seal and spread it onto a biscuit. Steam pours out of the dough when I pull it apart, burning my fingers.

"Maybe so, but you're still doing it," Hannah says. "How long have you been in love with Beckett?"

"I'm not," I say a little quicker than I intended.

Tay has been telling me I'm in love with him nonstop lately, and I haven't gotten upset over it. Maybe now I am because I'm finally starting to believe it. My feelings for Beckett run deeper than a crush or physical attraction, and it scares the hell out of me.

"Sorry, I didn't mean to sound harsh. I just... God, I'm sorry. I don't know what's wrong with me."

"Hey, it's okay. I get it." Hannah reaches across the table and places her hand on my wrist, picking up on my discomfort. I'm suddenly thankful she chose a restaurant outside of town where no one knows us. "What scares you the most?"

"That's easy," I say without having to think about it. "Losing him. He has been in my life longer than I can remember. I can't imagine it without him."

She watches me thoughtfully, tightening her grip. "Then don't you think your bond runs deeper than one mistake? I mean, I hardly know you, let alone Beckett, but from what I saw last night, I think he'll always be in your life, Mac. One way or another."

I nod, afraid my voice will crack if I speak. I've never talked about Beckett with anyone before. *He's* the one I go to for everything, but I can't get advice about my feelings for him *from* him. Until this week, I couldn't even admit them to myself.

Hannah seems to get it, though. "Thanks, Hannah."

"Don't worry about it." She removes her hand from my wrist, then she mirrors my exact thoughts from last night. "And if it's any consolation, *friends* don't dance like that."

Hannah and I talked for a while longer, and it was refreshing. I feel a little lighter from her advice, and I think about it throughout my shift at the diner. My boss, Pete, showed up halfway through and told me to head home since business was slow, and when I still haven't heard from Beckett two hours before the barbecue, I decide to text him.

The best thing I can do is pretend everything is normal until I see him in person later.

Me: *Are you going to the barbecue?*

He starts typing almost immediately, and my stomach flips.

Beckett: *Crap, that's tonight?*

Okay, this is normal. That was a normal response. Everything is fine.

Me: *Yeah, Hannah reminded me. Gabe asked her to go with him.*
Beckett: *When did you see Hannah?*
Me: *She asked me to get brunch.*

I brace myself, then send another message.

Me: *Do you want a ride down together?*
Beckett: *Carlyle's place is at the bottom of the hill, so I'm going to walk.*

The bubbles at the bottom of the screen shimmy, pending another message. Then they disappear, and my hopes plummet.

We've never gone separately to a *single* town function. In fact, when one of us can't go to something, neither of us do.

A few seconds later, the bubbles reappear, and another message comes through.

Beckett: *If you want to.*

If I want to? Does he mean if I want to walk with him?

Me: *Sounds good. It's a nice day anyway.*

It's a nice day? Tell me I didn't just bring up the weather.

Beckett: *Meet at your place around five?*

That's right when the barbecue starts. He always comes over well before we do anything, and I want to tell him to come sooner, but I don't have a reason for him to. We'll be eating there, so I can't suggest ordering food before we go.

Except, when have I ever needed a reason to invite Beckett over? All we do is *nothing* together. I'm overthinking this.

Me: *I'm home, so you can come over whenever.*
Maybe sneak a few beers before we go.

I'm fully prepared for him to make an excuse to avoid spending time with me, but then his next message thrusts my heart out of my chest and makes me want to hurl at the same time.

Beckett: *See you in thirty.*

True to his word, Beckett shows up thirty minutes

later, using the front door since my parents are still at work.

I've done my best to avoid them the last few days, and I haven't seen either of them for more than a few seconds at a time.

It's better to avoid someone completely than repeatedly lie to their face. At least, that's what I'm going with.

"Question—" Beckett says, dropping down on my bed. I'm in front of the dresser mirror, sticking the posts of dangling earrings through my lobes. "How many beers is appropriate before going to a town barbecue?"

I hum thoughtfully, glad our first conversation is in typical fashion of our friendship. "That depends on whether you want your buzz to last for the duration of the night."

"Fair point. So, six?"

"Four," I counter. "You get too hyper after six, and there's no way I'm carrying you up this damn hill if you drink too much."

"You're no fun," he pouts, and I can feel his eyes on me as I brush my hair over my shoulder to put in the other earring.

"You know I'm right," I singsong, watching as he uses his shirt to twist the cap off a beer, exposing the entire right half of his tan stomach.

He must feel my stare because he glances up, but I look away and walk toward my nightstand, snatching the beer out of his hand in the process.

I take a long swig and lift my phone before peering over my shoulder. "Thanks for opening that for me."

He gapes, reaching to grab my elbow and yank me toward him. "You said you didn't want one yet."

"I changed my mind." I giggle as I thrash against him and trip backward, stumbling over his lap and almost falling to the floor. He catches me around the waist, holding me to his chest as I attempt to break free. I switch hands and hold the beer as far away from him as I can when he reaches for it.

"Get your own!" I yell, laughing as he tries to balance me on his thighs and force my arm toward him by tugging on my sleeve.

"I *did*," he argues as he pinches my side, causing me to yelp and almost drop the bottle. "Give it back."

"Uh-uh." I refuse, and he abandons his efforts to start tickling me instead.

I shriek and bring my elbows in tight to compress his wiggling fingers. He takes advantage of the moment and grabs the neck of the bottle, but I refuse to let go, rolling to the side so fast he loses his grip. I jump to my feet and swing open the bedroom door, bolting downstairs and stumbling over the last few steps.

Beckett's a lot faster than me, so by the time my feet land on the hardwood, he's all but caught up to me. I skid through the kitchen and into the adjoining living room, circling the couch and stopping in front of the TV.

I've backed myself into a corner and he's right on my tail.

Knowing it's over for me, I make a split-second

decision and bring the bottle to my lips. I take several long gulps before he seizes me from behind, one arm wrapping around my stomach and the other grappling for the drink.

I choke on my laughter, and cold beer dribbles down my chin as I chug the remainder and release a loud belch.

Beckett is laughing so hard that he has to rest his chin on my shoulder to catch his breath. "God, MacKenzie, have some class."

I cough into my sleeve and then wipe it along my chin, chest burning from the carbonation, laughter, and physical exertion. "You're the reason it came to this."

"No, *you* started it when you stole my damn drink," Beckett grits, rocking me back and forth like he wants to shake the beer out of me. "I've never met someone so frustrating in my entire life."

"She gets that from her mother."

My eyes bulge, and Beckett releases me immediately, putting a foot of space between us as though we're not allowed to touch despite the whole town thinking we're getting married.

"Dad. Hi. How long have you...?"

"Just long enough to witness my underage daughter chug a beer in under seven seconds," he says, but there's a wry smile on his lips, so at least I know he's not mad.

"I had to," I explain, still breathless. "Beckett was trying to take it from me."

Beckett slaps my arm with the back of his hand, voice raising an octave. "It was *my* beer."

Then my dad asks the most logical question anyone could in this moment. "Was it the only one left?"

Beckett and I glance at each other, and it occurs to me that all he had to do was open another bottle for himself, but he didn't. He tugged me into his lap and chased me through the house, just like he did when we were kids—sans the beer.

"It wasn't about the beer, sir," he says seriously. "It was about what the beer stood for."

"Oh, and what would that be?" I challenge.

Beckett purses his lips, trying to devise a response. "... respect?"

I wave the bottle in front of him. "My house. My beer."

"My money. My consumption," he retorts with a satisfied smirk. I can't exactly argue with that when I need him to supply the booze since he's two years older.

"Mac, can I talk to you for a second?" Dad asks, clearing his throat.

I move around Beckett, touching his forearm briefly. "I'll meet you upstairs?"

He glances between me and my dad with a nod. "Yeah, sure. I'll see if I can't stake claim on a beer of my own."

I roll my eyes and walk toward my dad, waiting until I hear my bedroom door close to talk. "You're not mad about the beer, are you?"

He snorts. "You think I don't know the two of you have been drinking on that balcony since you were fifteen?"

My lips part in a sheepish grin. There's no sense arguing the truth; if he was angry about it, he would have grounded me five years ago.

"It took me a while to figure out why I kept finding empty beer bottles in the yard. Then I realized they were blowing off your balcony." He laughs with mild amusement before growing serious again.

"You never said anything."

"There were worse places and people you could have been drinking with. I figured the balcony with your best friend was the best I could ask for."

He has a point. As far as being a reclusive child goes, my tendencies were mild. "Then what did you want to talk about?"

"I just want you to be careful is all," he says, eyes drifting toward the stairs Beckett ascended moments ago.

"Careful?" I falter, taken aback by his concern. "I thought you liked Beckett...?"

"I do, he's a good kid. It's not that." He pauses. "I grabbed breakfast at the diner before work today."

I'm confused for a moment until I remember who was scheduled for the morning shift. "What did she say to you?"

Dad shakes his head, and I feel nauseous. "Tay didn't say anything *to me*, but I overheard her talking to someone on the phone about your—" he lifts his hands to make air quotes, "—engagement."

I shut my eyes. He must be so disappointed in me. "Dad, I—"

He shakes his head again, and I don't think he has the slightest clue how to deal with this. "I'm not going to pretend to understand why you'd feel the need to lie about being engaged, and I'm not going to make you tell me. I just want to make sure you know what you're doing."

My heart is heavy in my chest. "Who else heard her?"

"I was the only one eating at the counter, so likely no one. I only saw two other people in the hour I was there, but that girl has a big mouth, Mac. Be careful."

"I will," I whisper. "I'm sorry for lying. It's... kind of a long story."

"Well, unless you plan on coming clean to the whole town, you need Tay to straighten hers out."

In agreement, I retreat upstairs with my heart pounding and head swimming with doubts.

Who the hell would Tay be talking on the phone to about me?

A naïve part of me wants to assume it was Hannah and forget about it, but if it wasn't, then that means she told someone else that Beckett and I aren't engaged. And if my dad overheard her, who knows who else might have.

In my room, I pull my phone out and type a message to her.

Me: *Who else besides Hannah knows about me and Beckett? My dad overheard you on the phone this morning at the diner. I didn't tell you so you could gossip to everyone in town, Tay.*

Beckett's on the balcony, and he must sense my change in mood because he stands from a folding chair and comes inside, offering me some of his beer. "What's wrong? Is he mad about us drinking?"

I squeeze my eyes shut like I'm in pain. "He knows we're not engaged."

When I open my eyes, Beckett's are wide. "Shit, that's worse than the beer."

"You think?" I press the heels of my palms into my eye sockets, and he wraps a hand around my wrists to push them down. He holds them between us, dipping his chin to look at me.

"How did he find out?"

I blink rapidly, in utter disbelief. "How do you think? Tay. She freaking told Hannah last night, too. And now, my dad overheard her telling someone else on the phone. This is all my fault. I never should have trusted her."

"Her actions are not your fault, Mac," he says, sliding his palm down my wrist and to my hand, then up my forearm and back again. "Do you have any idea who else she might have told?"

"No." I meet his concerned eyes. "She knows so many people, I wouldn't know where to start. I just texted her about it."

"I'm sure it's fine. Maybe she was talking to Hannah."

I flatten my lips doubtfully. "Becks, if people find out this entire engagement is fake, we'll never live it down."

"I know," he sighs, looking a little worse for wear. "If my mom finds out, she'll be crushed. A broken engagement is one thing, but finding out that we're not —" He pauses like he's not sure how to finish his thought, then completely skips over the detail. "She absolutely adores you. I think she likes you more than me, actually."

"I like her more than you, too," I mumble, quirking my lips to the side with a tiny shrug.

He fights a smirk. "You know, that really hurt."

"Your ego?" I ask.

"No." He flattens my palm over his heart, pressing my fingers into his chest muscles. "Can you feel that?"

I raise an eyebrow. "Are you really looking for validation on your pecs?"

"Well, I *wasn't*. I was just going to ask if you could feel where your insult broke my heart. However, if you have something to say about my muscles, I wouldn't be opposed to a compliment."

"Oh, a *compliment?*" I bite my lip awkwardly. "I don't have anything good to say."

Beckett chuckles, and my phone buzzes where I set it on the dresser. I groan my discontentment, knowing it's most likely Tay.

"Come here," Beckett says, and I step into him, sliding my arms around his waist and resting my head on his chest. His beer presses against my back, and I melt into him. "We'll figure it out."

"I know," I mumble, though I'm not sure if he's talking about Tay or whatever's going on between us that we're too scared to address.

All I know is his arms feel like home, and I've never felt so secure as when I'm in them.

My phone buzzes again after two minutes, but Beckett holds me against him so I can't check it. He shifts to set his bottle on the dresser and picks it up instead.

"What did she say?" I ask, afraid of the answer.

He doesn't respond right away, and I feel the muscles in his forearm flexing as his thumb moves across the keyboard. After a minute, he tilts the screen toward me so I can read Tay's message and the reply he typed out but hasn't sent.

Tay: *Ahh, my bad! I'll be more careful!*
Me: *We'd rather you stop talking about it altogether. I told you the truth in confidence, you have no right to tell anyone else.*

"Send it." I give my approval. "It's almost five. We should probably start walking to Carlyle's."

"Sounds good," he says, and I back out of his grasp, immediately feeling the loss of his arms.

I gesture toward my closet. "I have to change real quick. I'll meet you out front."

Before he can leave, Tay texts back, and Beckett reads the message over my shoulder.

Tay: *Don't sweat it—you're coming to the barbecue tonight, right? I have a big surprise planned ;)*

"Don't worry about her," he says. "We're going to have fun like we always do."

Then he surprises me by pulling me in for another hug. This time, his arms circle my waist, and I bend my elbows around his neck, standing on my tiptoes and leaning into him for balance.

He brushes a kiss to the side of my head before releasing me, and the sentiment makes me so dizzy I have to latch onto his triceps for support.

The room temperature rises ten degrees when I lift my gaze to his, but he backs away casually, shooting me a grin as he slips out of my bedroom.

"Don't forget the beer."

I sit on my bed for a moment and drop my head in my hands to withhold a scream.

Beckett Harlow is going to be the death of me.

I swear he felt something last night, but then he kisses me on the side of the head like it's nothing and it makes me doubt everything.

Am I only seeing what I want to? Am I projecting my feelings onto simple acts he's always done because I want them to mean more?

Once a minute has passed and I've composed myself, I grab a shapely, navy blue tee and pair it with a pair of boyfriend jeans, tying a blue and white flannel around my waist in case I get cold later. Then I grab the beer and my house keys before jogging downstairs to meet Beckett outside.

Chapter Ten

TEN MINUTES LATER, Beckett and I are sticky with sweat and panting from the walk down the hill. If the humidity doesn't subside at sundown, it's going to be a brutal night.

He extends his arm toward me, and I hand him my empty beer bottle, which he discreetly deposits into the Martins' dumpster as we pass, along with two of his own.

His gray shirt is soaked and adhered to his back, and I find my eyes tracing his lat muscles before I realize what I'm doing. He glances back when I lag, and I scrunch my nose as a cover, pinching the material on his lower back and pulling it away from his skin. "You're disgusting."

"Right, and that's just your natural glow the sun's reflecting on," he retorts, eyeing my sticky face and arms.

I wipe the sweat from my upper lip, squinting with disdain. "You're damn right."

He snorts, passing me the water bottle he stole from

my house. Though, at this rate, I'd rather splash it on my face than drink it. Still, I tip the bottle up, taking two large gulps before handing it back to him.

The heat's bad enough, but the beers we drank didn't help with hydration.

"What should we say if someone asks how long we've been together?" I ask, eyeing Carlyle's house up ahead. "And what about Tay? We need to figure out how to shut her up."

"I don't think anyone will ask," Beckett says, shoulder bumping into mine as he walks, watching the gravel. "As for Tay, maybe we need to convince *her* that we're together. Then she won't have anything to gossip about."

I doubt that's true. If anything, she'll tell even more people we lied, then claim she's the reason we got together.

Then again, maybe if she thinks we're really dating, she'll grow bored of this charade.

"Maybe," I relent, and we slow our pace as we reach the barbecue.

Music and voices sound off the neighboring houses, and I peer between them, catching glimpses of kids running around the yard with water balloons and squirt guns. "I still think we need a cover story for everyone else. The townsfolk may be wondering what took us so long to get together, but you've had so many girlfriends over the years, including four in the past two months, that if anyone stops to think about it, the timeline won't add up."

"Look, if anyone asks, I'll just say that despite every

118

girl I've ever dated, it's always been you. No one will question that." He takes my hand and leads me in the direction of Carlyle's sweet-smelling barbecue. "And if you *really* want to convince Tay we're together, we could just settle on a lounge chair and make out all night."

"Go to hell," I laugh, tucking my hair behind my ear. "You better watch yourself, or one of these days I just might lay one on you to shut you up."

Beckett's lips quirk. "Who says that hasn't been my plan all along?"

I have no idea how to respond to that, so I scan the yard, taking in the dozens of families talking, laughing, and drinking around the lawn and patio. Many litter the lawn furniture, some jump in the pool, and others merely watch their kids chase each other around the yard with amused smiles. I'm reminded of when Beckett and I used to be those kids, screeching and stumbling over our feet.

The summer when I was nine, I tripped over the hose and face-planted on the grass. I'd cried instantly, and Mrs. Harlow rushed to my aid, chastising Beckett for chasing me when it wasn't his fault. I was the one who dared him to catch me.

Still, she forced him to apologize, and he kissed my cheek and told me he was sorry anyway.

Of course, back then, the last thing I wanted was a *boy* to kiss me.

Instead of acknowledging his comment, I nudge him with my shoulder and gesture to the barrel of water balloons to his left. "What do you say, Becks? Want to chase me around the yard for old-time's sake?"

"Mac, I've been chasing you around just about every day of my life," he says tiredly, hand tightening on mine as he reaches to the side and grabs a small water balloon. "Maybe it's time you stop running from me."

My eyes widen, and I try to pull away. "No. No, no, no—"

He swings the balloon, popping it on my chest.

"You *asshole*," I seethe, gaping down at the front of my wet shirt. "I can't believe you just did that."

I wrench out of his grasp and lunge for the water balloons, but two long strides are all it takes for him to catch me around the waist and pull me back.

As a kid runs by, I snatch a large water gun out of his hand, point it over my shoulder, and squirt Beckett straight in the face. He jerks backward, and I spin around, dousing his face and torso in water until he's sopping wet.

When the gun is empty, I turn toward the boy I stole it from. "Sorry, kid. Here you go."

His expression is one of pure shock, but then a large grin creeps over his face. "That was *awesome!*"

He holds up a hand for me to high five, then runs across the yard to grab the hose and refill his toy.

I watch the water drip off Beckett, delighted by his misery. "Now what have we learned?"

Beckett's jaw tics, and he ruffles his hair before smoothing it back.

"That you were a better sport when you were nine," he grumbles, squeezing out his shirt next.

"Truce?" I offer, puffing out my bottom lip and extending my hand.

He takes it reluctantly. "It feels like you're luring me into a false sense of security."

"Oh, just look at you two!" Beverly, a diner regular, sashays toward us, pulling me in for a hug before squeezing Beckett's cheeks affectionately. She can't very well hug him with how wet he is. "You're too precious. I couldn't believe the news when I heard. Though, I wasn't surprised, either." She turns to Beckett, taking his hands. "I was just talkin' to your momma, and she is beyond ecstatic about the two of you. Couldn't stop gushin' about how cute her grandbabies will be."

I choke on my saliva and search the crowd for potential escape routes, but Beckett's fingers slide between mine, swallowing my hand in his as Beverly continues rambling.

"So, we were talkin' and thought, 'wouldn't it just be marvelous to have a nice big dinner to celebrate?' Everyone loves you, might as well make it a grand celebration. Speakin' of—have you set a date yet?"

My tongue feels three times its size when I open my mouth.

"We're waiting until after I graduate to work out the specifics," Beckett says easily, and his thumb strokes mine in a soothing motion as he speaks. "Trying to plan a wedding while I'm ten hours away in Boston wouldn't be fair to either one of us. Besides, we're not in any rush."

"Ahh, I see." She wags her finger at him with a sneaky smile. "You just wanted to lock this pretty girl down before you left."

"You caught me." Beckett laughs uncomfortably, and when it's clear he doesn't know what else to say, I step in.

"Can you blame him?" I joke, causing Beverly to throw her head back with the sweetest laugh. "If he hadn't, Bill and Marv might've swept me off my feet while he was gone. He had to do something."

Beverly laughs even harder, as Bill and Marv are two eighty-something regulars at the diner. Both single, both with an affinity for younger women.

"There's Gabe and Hannah," Beckett says, pointing to the right. "Will you excuse us? It was wonderful to see you, Beverly."

"You, too, sweetheart." She kisses his cheek and strokes my hair. "You two take care of each other now. I'll see you at that engagement dinner."

Beckett releases my hand and slides his palm across my back as we head in Hannah and Gabe's direction. There's a faraway look in Beckett's eyes, but he doesn't have to say it—I know exactly what he's thinking.

He feels dirty.

Beverly is the sweetest woman alive, just like Beckett's mom. She's not nosy like most of the townsfolk, and she genuinely cares despite only seeing us in brief increments over the years.

She doesn't deserve to be duped by our lie.

One thing neither of us took into consideration is the scrutiny we'll receive when we call this off. There was a point when I thought no one would believe the two of us were in a relationship, but now, I worry no one will understand how we could ever break up.

"I know," I whisper, leaning into his side as we walk. "A few more weeks."

His tongue darts over his lips as he stares ahead, guiding us through the crowd. "I don't know if I can pretend that long."

I look up at him, surprised to find myself saddened by the prospect. "You want to call it off sooner?"

He meets my gaze, staring for a long moment before he shakes his head. "That's not what I meant."

"Then what?" I ask, saying hello to a few family friends as we pass. Several of them congratulate us, and with every genuine smile, I feel more and more like a fraud.

"Doesn't matter," Beckett says, fingers pulsing around my hip as we near our friends. "Like you said, only a few more weeks and everything will go back to the way it was."

The way it was.

When Beckett didn't have an excuse to touch me in public, so he rarely did.

When he's away at college and I'm stuck here without the only person I want to spend every second of every day with, working a job with no future.

The last thing I want is to go back to the way things were. I'm tired of standing still.

Hannah's face lights up when she sees us, and her almond eyes flit to Beckett's arm around me. She's wearing a brown romper with pink and blue flowers, and platform sandals that match perfectly. "You made it!"

She gives me a half hug, releasing Gabe's hand. He's wearing a black t-shirt, and his hair is gelled back, styled more nicely than the usual blob that curtains over his forehead.

"Barely," I remark. "It was touch-and-go walking down the hill."

"You walked here in this heat?" Hannah asks, floored.

Beckett nods as he pulls the water bottle out of his back pocket, taking a swig before offering it to me. I decline, indicating he can finish it.

"Anyone want a drink?" Gabe offers, tipping three travel-sized bottles of Grey Goose out of his pocket. "I figured we could make our own adult fruit punch since the old geezers won't spike ours."

Beckett's shoulders shake with laughter, and the two of them head to the drink table to pour us cups of the fruit punch labeled 'For the Kiddos.'

I moisten my lips, watching Beckett's arm move between the punch bowl and the cups Gabe set in front of him.

"Earth to MacKenzie," Hannah singsongs, elbowing me lightly.

I rip my eyes from Beckett, cheeks heating. "Sorry, what?"

She smirks. "Never mind, it's not important."

"Yes, it is," I say, face pinched with guilt. "I'm listening now."

Hannah waves me off like it's no big deal. "I said that

Tay texted earlier to invite me tonight—she has no idea me and Gabe are hanging out. Anyway, I didn't know if you knew she was coming."

Dread forms in my gut. "Yeah, I had to text her earlier. My dad overheard her talking about the fake engagement on the phone."

Hannah cups a hand over her mouth. "Mac, you're kidding. I'm so sorry."

"It is what it is, I guess." I shrug, knowing that's just one of the many consequences of our lie. *And* of trusting Tay. "She said she has a surprise planned for tonight."

"Any idea what it could be?"

"No, but her big mouth is getting on my last nerve."

"That's a nice way of saying she's a nosy, meddlesome bitch," Hannah remarks, not looking the least bit apologetic.

I scrunch my nose. "I'm pretty sure that's also a nice way to describe her."

Gabe reappears with three Solo cups while Beckett gets himself a beer from the adult beverage table since he's the only one of age.

Hannah and I each take a drink, and Gabe moves closer, unscrewing the cap of a Grey Goose shooter. "Cover me."

We huddle around him while he pours a shot into his and Hannah's glasses.

"I'm good right now," I say, not in the mood for a mixed drink.

"All right, let me know if you change your mind. I'm

going to get rid of the evidence," he says, eyeing a trashcan on the patio. "Be right back."

"Grab some spoons, would you?" Hannah asks with a sour expression. "All of the vodka is on top."

Gabe nods and conspicuously moves toward the garbage can to discard the empty bottles. Although, I doubt a single adult here would give us a second glance if we were seen with alcohol.

"He's such a dork," Hannah says, watching him with a little smile on her face.

Beckett appears beside me and taps his beer can to her glass, then mine. "I can drink to that."

"To Gabe being a dork," I announce, just as the man himself returns with two spoons. I gulp the zesty fruit punch, scrunching my nose.

"What are we toasting?" he asks, sticking a spoon in Hannah's cup.

She kisses his cheek, and he blushes. "You, of course."

I dump my drink in the grass and pluck Beckett's from his hand, pouring a quarter of the beer into my empty cup.

He shoots me a crooked grin, then takes my cup and pours the rest of his beer in it before crushing the can against his stomach with a wink.

He leans close, lips brushing my ear. "I know better. I'll get another one."

I hold my breath until he backs toward the beverage table, suddenly dizzy.

This is going to be a long night if he doesn't keep his hands off me.

For the remainder of the evening, we stick with Hannah and Gabe, making small talk with whoever comes to congratulate us on the engagement. Beckett does most of the talking, careful to keep details of our "romantic life" general whenever anyone asks.

He was right earlier, though—very few people pry for specifics because they've suspected we were more than friends all along.

As the night ages, nearing eleven o'clock, I find myself growing more relaxed and easing into the role of Beckett's fiancée. Strangely enough, besides the initial guilt of lying, it's not all that awkward. Not to mention, I don't entirely hate listening to him describe our relationship in more intimate parameters, like we've been in love all these years.

The crowd thins a bit as some of the older residents head home, but if this is like every other year, the party isn't nearly over.

Tay showed up earlier while Beckett and I were getting food, but she hasn't come to say hello yet, absorbed by every conversation someone pulls her into. I've kept my back to her, afraid the slightest acknowledgment will compel her over here. With any luck, she's noticed Beckett's constant physical touch and has abandoned her desire to meddle.

His hand moves absently across my back as he speaks, deep in conversation with Gabe and Hannah, discussing his finance classes in Boston for the upcoming semester.

I merely listen since I already know everything there is about his education, waiting patiently for an opening to broach the subject of leaving. The heat and constant conversation have worn me out, and now that my buzz has faded, I'm beyond exhausted. It doesn't help that I hardly slept last night.

More than anything, I want to lie across my bed, watch an action rom-com with my best friend, and fall asleep midway through, knowing that he won't leave until I wake up.

"Hold on a second," Gabe says, pulling me out of my thoughts. His phone is ringing, and he steps away, waving the device in the air. "My sister's calling."

Hannah follows, taking his drink so he has both hands to answer the call.

"Can you take my beer? I'm going to run to the bathroom real quick," Beckett says.

"Yeah, sure," I say, but he holds it out of reach.

"Take it to *hold* for me. *Not* to finish."

I pout, reaching past him and wrapping my hand around the can. "You're no fun."

My gaze travels over him as he strides toward the portable restrooms at the far end of the yard, which are set up so the entire town isn't using Carlyle's powder room. I watch him shamelessly, not the least bit concerned someone might catch me since we're supposed to be in love anyway.

The second he's gone, someone runs up behind me

and grabs my shoulders, jerking me so hard I almost drop Beckett's beer. A little splashes over the lip and onto my legs, and I turn to glare at the culprit.

"Good Lord, I thought he'd never leave your side," Tay says, bouncing on her toes while taking a sip from a red cup that I doubt came from the "kiddo" punch bowl. She's wearing a white crop top and a light blue mini skirt that rides up so often she has to pull it down every other second.

"Tay, I'm not in the mood," I say, bringing Beckett's beer to my lips because I have a feeling I'll need it here in a minute.

She rolls her eyes. "Mac, I'm trying to help you."

"And I told you, I don't need it." I do my best to keep my tone light. If I learned anything about her at the bar, it's that she doesn't respond to frustration. "Things are actually really good between me and Beckett."

"Whatever you have to tell yourself," she says, not bothering to hide her doubt as she scans the crowd, pensive eyes searching for something. "You remember Kim, don't you?"

Think happy thoughts, Mac.

"Mmhmm."

"Well, I realized that pushing you on Beckett was never going to get you to admit you're in love with him. *However*, forcing your hand might." A mischievous grin stretches her lips. "But then I realized Kim wasn't the answer. She's a one-nighter and everyone knows it. Plus, she likes the challenge, and a man who isn't *really* engaged wouldn't be worth her efforts."

"What did you do?" I ask, sucking on my teeth.

"Look—over there." She points, and I strain to peer through the crowd. Some of the younger guests have started dancing now that the majority of adults are gone, so it's hard to see with them bouncing around.

Then my eyes catch on a familiar, curvy brunette talking to Beckett. She's wearing a strapless maroon dress that cuts midway down her chest, so her cleavage projects upward when she stands straighter.

"She drove in from the city to visit her family and attend the barbecue. I heard she was upset that Beckett moved on so quickly, so..."

"You told Lainey the truth," I realize, blood boiling. Lashing out means she wins, and I have to remind myself of that as I take two large gulps of beer.

Tay remains unapologetic. "She doesn't like losing, and she wants him back."

"She didn't want him a week ago," I grit.

But now that she knows I don't have him... he's fair game.

"Relax. I just encouraged her to shoot her shot with Beckett. She doesn't even know the plan is for *you* to swoop in and confess your undying love for him." Tay sways on her feet, and I have no idea if she's drunk, or just that pleased with herself. "Now, are you going to stand there like some lovesick fool, or are you going to mark your territory?"

Beckett glances my way, but Lainey puts her hand on his arm, drawing his attention back to her. She wants to tempt him.

Regardless, I won't give Tay or Lainey the satisfaction of causing a scene. They want me to feel inferior, but the truth is, if Beckett was really my fiancé, if he was really loyal to me, I wouldn't have to worry about a thing.

Tay sighs heavily. "Mac—"

"This is the last time I'm going to tell you this," I say firmly, giving her a hard look. "Stay out of my business. Stay away from me and Beckett. And stop trying to interfere with our relationship. What we are to each other is no concern of yours, and your master plan to get us together stops now."

Several people block my view of Beckett, and I desperately pray that he told Lainey to screw off already.

Except, why would he? We're not together. He's technically free to flirt with whomever he wants.

Besides... wasn't this the plan all along?

Tay eyes me pitifully. "Girl, without me, you'd still be pining over him. Not dancing body to body at the bar or—"

"You have no right to meddle in my life, and if you keep at it, you might ruin my friendship with Beckett, much less any chance we have at dating. If I want him, I'll tell him on my terms and not because of your schemes."

"Is everything all right?" Hannah moves to my side, eyes skating between Tay and me.

Tay smiles brightly, giving Hannah a half hug. "Everything's just fine." Then she turns back to me, and it seems my irritation has finally registered because she's lost her playful edge. "He has to realize how he feels about you, and you need to admit that you're in love with him."

"No, I don't. *You* want me to. Besides, if he doesn't know how he feels about me, then maybe it's because he doesn't feel anything for me." My eyes drift back toward the swarm of bodies in search of Beckett.

Never in my life had I entertained the idea that he might view me as more than a friend someday, and right when I let myself dream, Tay waltzes in with his gorgeous ex who would love nothing more than to steal him away from me just to prove that she can.

The crowd parts slightly, and I catch sight of Beckett and Lainey. He's turning away from her, but her slender hand seizes his, stopping him. He turns over his shoulder as she says something, then she presses against him, places a hand on his cheek, and kisses him before I can process what's happening.

I refrain from watching what happens next, heart aching at the image of her lips on his.

"He pushed her away," Hannah says, for my ears only. But I'm already backing away, pushing his drink at her.

"Not soon enough."

"Mac, you're not hearing me." Hannah catches my hand before I can flee. "He didn't kiss her back. He was caught off guard, but he pushed her off right away."

I nod, then I mumble an excuse to leave, tripping over my feet as I cut through the crowd, between the houses, and head straight for the road.

I'm only a few feet up the hill when I hear footsteps

pounding on the sidewalk, followed by Beckett calling my name. "Mac, wait."

Turning, I force a strained smile as he reaches me. He stops so close that I step backward on reflex. He purses his lips, but all I can see is Lainey's on them. It feels like a piece of me died when they shared breath.

"Sorry, I, uh..." I hug my waist and clear my throat. "I'm just so tired. I had to leave."

I hate that I feel like crying.

I hate *myself*.

He may have stopped the kiss, and I don't blame him for it, but witnessing it made me realize how delusional I've been.

More than anything, I'm *embarrassed*.

I'm embarrassed because, for one minute, I let myself believe he could have feelings for me, too.

"Is that really why you left?" he asks, running a hand through his hair.

What does he expect me to do? Confess that I left because I'm pathetic and jealous and so utterly in love with him that the thought of him kissing someone else makes me feel like I'm dying?

Maybe I should. Maybe I should just lay it all out there.

Except, I'm too afraid that if I admit the truth, I'll not only get rejected, but I'll lose him forever. I also don't know how to let these feelings go or how to be around him every day when I feel this way.

I swallow my emotions. "Yeah, you looked like you were having fun, and I didn't want to bother you."

"I was having fun with *you*." He reaches for me, but I step away again, and he drops his hand, looking as though he has no idea what to do. "Hannah said that you saw—" He closes his eyes. "Mac, she kissed me before I knew what was happening."

"Yeah, I know," I say, trying my best to sound indifferent. "Like you said, I saw."

He shifts his weight. "Right."

"It's not like we're together. So..."

His tongue slides over his bottom lip, followed by his teeth. "We're still supposed to be engaged. It would look bad if anyone saw."

Finally, I see things clearly.

I see this for what it is.

"Well, if that's all you're worried about." I can't hide the bite in my voice, and I'm not entirely sure I want to. He's standing here, failing at apologizing for kissing someone, and all I want is to believe it's more than an obligation.

Every second I stare at him costs me another shard of my heart.

"Mac, I'm sorry."

"I get it. Really. We're not together, Beckett. This is exactly what you wanted—it's why we're doing this in the first place."

I force another smile and start back up the hill, but he calls after me with two simple words that stop me in my tracks.

"Is it?"

So, I turn back around with a limp shrug, arms swaying at my sides as I take in all six feet of him.

"Why else?" I ask, daring, begging, pleading with him to declare the truth. To admit there's something between us and he's known it all along.

He just stares at me, speechless, and I nod stiffly before turning to head home, leaving him standing on the sidewalk. "That's what I thought."

By the time I throw the front door open, my face is wet with tears, but I don't truly let myself cry until I'm tucked safely in my room. I fall flat on my bed without bothering to turn the lights on, this way my parents won't see that I'm home early and wonder why.

Rolling onto my side, I wipe the tears from under my eyes as more fall, then bury my face in my hands.

I just *had* to fall in love with my best friend.

This was a bad idea from the start, and I knew it. But I couldn't stop myself from jumping at the chance to be with him, even if it was only pretend.

My phone vibrates in my back pocket, and I slip it out to find a text from Beckett.

Beckett: *Did you make it home okay?*

Wiping the tears off my fingers, I let him know that I'm home. As I swipe to close out of my texts, a phone call comes through, and I accidentally answer.

Cursing silently, I peer at my brother's name across the screen.

"Mac? You there?" Ryan asks when I don't say anything right away.

"Hey, yeah. I'm here. I'm sorry I never called you back, things have been kind of crazy lately." I suck in a shaky breath, struggling to keep my voice even. "I appreciate you calling, but I'm really not in the mood to talk about the engagement right now. Can I call you back tomorrow?"

Ryan is silent for a moment. "The engagement? I didn't know you were seeing anyone."

More tears well in my eyes, but I force them down. "If you didn't call about Beckett, then what did you need?"

"Hold on, you're engaged to Beckett Harlow?" The shock in his voice is evident. He may have been absent for most of my life, but he'd have to live under a rock to not know Beckett.

"Why did you call me, Ryan?" I ask tiredly.

He's quiet for a moment, and I'm almost positive he's going to press me on the subject, but he doesn't. "Angela said you and I don't talk enough."

I blink several times. "So, you called to tell me...?"

He laughs, but it's strained. "Yes and no. After we got home from vacation, she and I had a long talk about it. I had my own life by the time you were six, but that's no excuse—I should have worked harder to build a relationship with you. Back then I was so focused on getting the hell out of Richlynd that I never stopped to highest

---

consider that I was leaving you behind to deal with the shit I was running from."

"I wasn't entirely alone," I say, if for nothing else than to make him feel better. "Beckett and his family were always there for me."

"Yes, and I'm grateful for them, but it doesn't change the fact that I wasn't. Now I have kids of my own and Angela said, 'Imagine how we'd feel if they hardly spoke to each other in twenty years.'" He pauses, and I let his words sink in. "I would never want that for them. I don't want that for us."

My chest swells, and the tears glazed over my eyes are for a different reason now. "Me neither."

"If you would want to visit Angela and me sometime before the summer ends, or anytime really, we'd love to have you. We'd come to you, but Ange and I both have full-time jobs and already took time off for the last vacation—"

"That would be great," I say earnestly. "I'd love the chance to get to know my niece and nephew better."

"They'd love that," he says. "We all would."

"I'm supposed to receive next month's schedule at the end of the week. I'll see if I can double up on some shifts and get a weekend off soon."

"Sounds good. Let me know what works."

I nod rapidly, even though he can't see me. "I will. Thanks for calling, Ryan."

"Of course. I'll talk to you soon."

We hang up, and I shift toward my headboard, wrapping my arms around a decorative pillow.

The despair I felt before lessened during our phone call, but even so, my chest still aches with the kind of raw pain only loving someone who doesn't love you back can induce.

In less than a week, my entire emotional infrastructure has been altered, and I don't know what I'll do if Beckett and I can't come back from this awkward state of uncertainty.

Deep down, I don't know that I want to.

Being his friend has slowly broken me down, and I'm afraid that as long as he's in my life, this yearning will never go away.

And yet, I love him too much to ever let him go.

I'd choose to suffer every day for the rest of my life if it meant keeping him in it.

If that's not the most self-sabotaging way of loving someone, I don't know what is.

Chapter Eleven

THE NEXT COUPLE days pass in a blur of chaste text conversations in which Beckett and I take turns inviting each other to hang out, only for the other to say they're too busy. Besides that, all we've spoken about are details regarding his parents' anniversary dinner, which I'm on my way to help with right now.

This is the longest we've ever gone without spending time together when we're in the same town, much less talking on the phone.

He hasn't called me once, and it's starting to sink in that there's an obvious tension between us that won't go away with ignorance. We both feel it, even if he doesn't know why.

I may have blown the kiss out of proportion, but it was also my opening to admit how I feel about him. The more I replay our conversation, the more I wonder if he was pushing me to do just that and I was too blinded by pain to see it.

When it comes down to it, I was upset because it was *me* I wanted him to kiss. Sure, he jokes about it constantly, but he has never come close to actually doing it.

Then something occurred to me while I thrashed around in my sheets late last night because I couldn't sleep: I've never witnessed him kiss a single one of his girlfriends in all the years I've known him.

Sure, he'd bring them around me, they'd hold hands, etc., but never has he so much as touched his lips to one of their cheeks in my presence.

I'm not sure why, but that thought is what I've focused on ever since.

A cluster of pent-up nerves swarm in my gut as I cross through his parents' yard.

Beckett left the garage door unlocked for me, and I slip inside, making my way up the creaky stairs to his apartment.

I'm not entirely sure how today will go, but I refuse to back out of helping him. His parents' anniversary is how this arrangement started, after all. The least I can do is see it through.

I knock twice, then hear his muffled voice holler to come in. I turn the knob with sweaty fingers and step inside the small apartment.

It's an open concept, so when I don't see him on the bed tucked into the alcove or at the kitchen counter, I assume he must be in the bathroom.

Moving past the bed, I head to the island parallel to

the stovetop and set down the bag of candles I lugged over here. Their glow, plus the poolside lights, will make for a beautifully romantic setting once it's dark out. It's the perfect evening for an outdoor dinner, too—not too sunny, with a nice breeze and low humidity.

The bathroom door opens to a puff of steam, and Beckett exits wearing nothing but a pair of sweatpants. There's a towel strung over his shoulders that absorbs the dollops of water dripping from his hair, and he lifts one end, wiping it down the side of his face.

"Hey," he says easily, walking past me to a closet off the kitchen and skimming through two-dozen hangers. He must not find what he's looking for because he abandons the clothes and heads to the alcove, sliding the towel off his neck and chucking it into a laundry basket on the floor.

"Sorry, I ran behind on lawn work today, and then it took me a while to find the recipe my mom wrote down when I was a kid." He rummages through what I hope is a clean basket of clothes on his bed.

"That's fine," I say, inhaling deeply.

The window beside his bed bathes half of his body with sunlight. My eyes move of their own accord, admiring the smooth grooves of his tan skin and the muscles that contract as he digs to the bottom of the basket.

He's acting casual, as though the barbecue never happened, but my heart won't let me revert to our default relationship that easily.

"The ingredients are on the counter if you want to boil water for the noodles. I preheated the oven already," Beckett says, then rotates around. I force my eyes to his face with great difficulty, refusing to let them wander as he slides his arms through a white button-down shirt.

Which he leaves unbuttoned.

He flattens the collar before tugging at the edges of his sleeves and rolling them midway up his forearms.

When I don't respond, too fixated on him, he glances up. "Or you could do something else...?"

"Like what?" I ask in a daze, then quickly catch myself.

He's asking if I'm against boiling the water. *Not* if I'd prefer to run my hands over his stomach instead.

"Uh, no. Water is... hot. *Good.* Water is good." I swallow. "I can boil water."

He eyes me strangely. "You sure about that?"

"Mmhmm." I head to the counter and scan the ingredients he laid out like they're the most interesting foods in the world—penne noodles, grated and shredded parmesan cheese, garlic powder, salt, pepper, thawed chicken, garlic, and olive oil.

I hold a pot under the faucet until it's halfway full and then place it on the burner, which I turn to high.

"I brought the candles," I say to make conversation, hoping I brought enough for what he has planned. His mom would have been suspicious if she caught him rummaging through the attic, so he asked me to supply them instead.

Beckett curses. "I forgot the matches."

Spinning around, I stick my fingers into the outside pocket of my bag and emerge with a pack of matches. "I figured you would."

I toss the pack his way, and he catches it easily, placing it over his heart with a lopsided grin. "You're the best."

"I know." I rest my tailbone against the counter, eyes boring holes into my fingernails while I wish he'd button his damn shirt.

If I have to deal with his bare chest all afternoon, I'll end up drooling on the meal.

"So, what do your parents think is going on tonight?"

He rakes a hand through his damp hair. "I told them we were going out to dinner at seven so they wouldn't make other plans. I figured we could wait until later to set up since it'll be more of a surprise if they don't see what we're up to."

Long strides carry him across the room, where he stops beside me to examine the unscented candles. His shoulder bumps mine as he sifts through the bag, and my breath hitches involuntarily.

The sound was soft.

So quiet that it was hardly audible.

And yet, it was still loud enough to make Beckett fumble with a candle before setting it firmly on the counter. He turns his head, blue eyes inspecting me as though searching for something deeper than the eye can see.

"Mac, I..." his voice trails off, but his gaze never wavers.

"Yeah?" I ask hoarsely, hands sweating where they grip the counter behind me.

Say it. Please, please say it so I know I'm not losing my mind.

His fingers brush my wrist, but his words don't seem to come.

The oven beeps, indicating it's preheated, but neither of us moves a muscle.

His throat bobs, and after a moment, he drops his gaze and removes his hand. "Lainey texted me yesterday."

And just like that, the excited hum beneath my skin progresses to a jealous simmer. "Lainey, huh? What did she want?"

He bows his neck, exhaling slowly. "Pretty much the same thing she said at the barbecue. She made a mistake breaking up with me and wants to meet for coffee to talk."

I remember the last time she wanted to *talk* to Beckett. It sure as hell involved her mouth.

"But you're supposed to be with me," I reason, then flounder in an attempt to clarify. "I mean, we're supposed to be engaged, right? Shouldn't she have some respect?"

"Tay told her we aren't engaged," Beckett says, as though that detail makes all the difference. I suppose it does. Since we haven't spoken about that night, he has no idea she told me.

"Right. Tay," I relent. "So, what does Lainey want to

talk about?" I place way too much emphasis on the word 'talk,' but it's too late to take it back now.

"She didn't say."

"Didn't she?" I ask futilely, focusing on the pot of water, which is slowly nearing the boiling point.

"No, she didn't," he repeats.

I swallow hard. "Are you going to go?"

"Should I?" he asks, moving to wash his hands in the sink before picking up the box of noodles.

I scream *no* over and over again in my head, but I can't force the word to my lips. I want to be the one he chooses, but I'm terrified of being the one who holds him back.

"If that's what you want," I wheeze, lungs constricting.

"Yeah," he says, mindlessly fiddling with the cardboard tab on the box. "Maybe."

"I guess you have your answer then."

He watches me for a moment, unreadable. "Yeah. I suppose I do."

We spend the rest of the evening speaking very little, and at one point, soon after we stop talking, he suggests I start setting up the table by the pool just to get rid of me.

I take my time, paying extra attention to the smoothness of the white tablecloth and the way the centerpiece candles are arranged. I even use a different match to light each of the ten candles just to waste time watching them burn down before lighting the next one.

By the time I return to the apartment, he's done cooking.

"It smells amazing," I say, setting my empty bag down.

Beckett gives a noncommittal grunt and scoops the pasta into two bowls, then cuts the chicken into strips and methodically places them on top of both dishes. Lastly, he garnishes the meal with parsley. "I have to get my parents onto the patio. Give me ten minutes and then carry down the food."

"'kay."

I'm almost certain he hasn't looked at me once since earlier, and I can't stand the tension between us.

I have no idea what he wants from me. For a second, I thought he might kiss me, or at least, I thought he was *thinking* about kissing me. Instead, he brought up Lainey and is now giving me the silent treatment.

What did he expect me to say?

Maybe the same thing you've been silently begging him to say for days?

"Becks?" I call after him, fisting my hands against my stomach.

He glances over his shoulder, already standing in the doorway, hand on the knob. His expression doesn't change.

"Never mind," I mumble, then begin searching for a tray to carry the bowls, silverware, and grated parmesan cheese on. I also rip off two paper towels to put over the food, that way bugs won't land on it while I walk across the yard.

When I look up, Beckett is long gone.

Ten minutes later, I carry the food out on a baking

tray that I found in one of the cabinets, cutting through the grass and pressing my back against the pool gate he left unlatched. I navigate the patio furniture until I reach the table where Mr. and Mrs. Harlow are now sitting in chairs opposite each other.

Her face lights up when she sees me, and she abandons a conversation with her husband to help me set the food down, then wraps me in a tight hug.

She's almost half my height at 4'10", so I have to bend down to hug her. The familiar scent of lavender and sandalwood fills my nostrils as I breathe in. I always liked Beckett's house more than my own, simply because everything smelled like happiness and warmth—the complete opposite of mine, which always felt empty and volatile.

"I ought to beat that boy of mine for making you carry all of this by yourself." She humphs in indignation, looking around the patio for Beckett, but he must have slipped away already. "Honey, this is beautiful. Thank you so much for doing this." She then slaps her husband, who laughs lightly, looking so much like Beckett when he does so.

He stands and pulls me into a hug as well. "My son is a lucky man. I always thought you were too smart to fall for a Harlow boy, but I underestimated his charm."

"Oh, don't tease the poor girl. She just slaved over a wonderful meal for us."

I force a smile. "Actually, dinner was all Beckett. I did, however, set the table."

"You did more than that." She holds up her arm to

draw attention to a chain link bracelet. I glance at her husband, who has a similarly styled watch clasped around his wrist. "Beckett gave us our gifts this morning. He said you picked them out."

"It's nothing, really," I insist. Mrs. Harlow beams at me, and when it's clear Beckett isn't coming back, I decide I'd better turn on the music and leave since he clearly doesn't want me here. "I'll let you enjoy your meal. Happy anniversary."

"Oh, wait—your momma called me this morning to wish us a happy anniversary," Mrs. Harlow says, taking her seat and removing the napkin from her bowl. "We both think it would be a wonderful idea to have dinner the Monday after next to celebrate your engagement. I know Beverly was talking about it, too."

"Yeah, she mentioned that. Sounds great," I lie cheerfully, dread expanding.

"We made reservations for seven at that nice restaurant outside of town. Malone's, I believe." She looks so pleased with herself that I don't have the heart to tell her no. "You're welcome to invite a few friends if you'd like."

"I'll think about it, thanks." I make my way onto the porch and inch toward the back door so I can turn on the Bluetooth speaker.

"MacKenzie?" Mrs. Harlow calls, and I halt, wanting nothing more than to get out of here.

"Next to the fridge is a wine rack, and on the bottom left is an unopened bottle of Cabernet Sauvignon from 1943. Would you bring it out for us?"

"Yeah, of course."

I walk through the sunroom off the porch and head directly toward the kitchen, where I seek out the wine rack. It's precisely where she said it would be, but I don't get a chance to look for the bottle because Beckett is leaning against the counter, scrolling through his phone.

His head jerks up when he hears me, but he doesn't say anything.

Determined to shut him out, I move toward the wine rack, but my frustration wins over my desire to wash this under the rug.

I've been avoiding a fight and ignoring my feelings because I'm scared of losing him. But at this rate, he's slipping away anyway.

I'd rather lose him because we're on different pages in our love lives than because we never discussed what we were feeling.

Closing my eyes, I turn to face him. "Becks, we can't keep doing this."

In all the years we've been friends, Beckett and I have never truly argued. Sure, we've had disagreements here and there, maybe someone took a joke a little too far and the other person gave them the silent treatment for an hour, but we've never actually fought.

"What do you mean?" He plays dumb, which only further infuriates me.

"You—you're being an asshole." The number of times I've called him that over the years is uncountable, but I can't think of a single time I meant it until tonight.

"I'm here to help you, and you're pretending I don't exist. Why are you mad at me?"

He sighs heartily, dragging a hand over his face. "I'm not mad at you."

There's less conviction in his voice than before, but I still don't believe him.

"You're lying," I say plainly.

"I'm not."

"Really? Because you've barely said two words to me all night."

He looks back at his phone like whatever's on there is more important than this conversation. Than me. "I'm just tired."

"So, you're not going to tell me? You're going to keep shutting me out and not tell me why?"

"I told you," he says calmly, still staring at his phone. "I'm not pissed. Just *tired*."

"Don't give me that. We once stayed up until five in the morning before your first day of football camp. It was ninety degrees, you wound up getting sick on the field, and you *still* called me after practice. You were exhausted and sore, but you wanted to talk to me," I say, my frustration increasing.

"Sorry, I didn't realize I had to talk to you every second of the day so you don't get insecure," he snaps, slapping his phone down on the counter. Regret flickers in his eyes, but he clenches his jaw, standing his ground instead of apologizing.

A pang of hurt surges through me, pricking my eyes and splitting my heart in two.

Is that honestly what he thinks of me? That I'm some needy, insecure woman who relies on his attention to feel like I have a purpose?

"You know, if that's what you think of me after all these years, then I have no idea why we're friends at all," I bite, holding back tears. I don't want him to see me cry, to know he hurt me, but judging by his stupefied expression, it's too late. "And to try and make me feel stupid, like I'm the one overreacting by asking if you're mad because you've blatantly ignored me and have been pretty freaking rude all night? I—"

"MacKenzie, did you find the wine?" Mrs. Harlow calls from the sunroom.

Beckett and I fall silent, staring at each other as if daring the other to speak first. After a beat, his mom's footsteps head in our direction, so I pull down the bottle of wine and grab two glasses from the cabinet before she reaches the kitchen.

"There you are. I was worried you couldn't find it," she says, then she takes me in, glancing from me to her son. "Is everything all right?"

"Yeah, of course," I say weakly, throat constricting. "I just forgot you keep the glasses above the oven now. I had to ask Beckett for help. Uhm, I'm actually supposed to be somewhere, so I have to go. But I hope you have a lovely anniversary, Mrs. Harlow."

Walking as swiftly as I can out of the kitchen, I speed across the patio and through the gate toward Beckett's apartment to get my stuff.

When I'm halfway through the patch of grass

between the Harlows' house and the garage, I can't hold back the hurt any longer. I cup my hand over my mouth to smother a sob as tears stream down my cheeks.

I can barely see through my bleary vision as I walk through his apartment. I grab my bag and sling it over my shoulder, accidentally sending my phone flying to the floor in the process.

Picking it up hastily, my feet propel me toward the door, but when I look up, Beckett is blocking it, looking at me like he just plowed over a chipmunk with his lawnmower.

He opens his mouth, but I cut him off before he can say a word.

"Just don't, okay?" I hardly recognize my voice.

I clench my fists around the strap of my bag and keep moving, prepared to shove him out of the way if he doesn't move.

His arm shoots out to block my path and I try to duck under it, but he lowers it to stop me.

"Mac." He says my name this time, and for a moment, neither of us moves as his eyes bore through me. He grazes my tear-stained cheek, the featherlight touch of his fingers holding all the strength in the world as he curls his extended arm around me and draws me into his arms.

"Don't," I choke, struggling to pull away as my tears fall faster.

Instead of complying, he kicks the door shut with his foot, slides the bag off my shoulder, and tosses my phone on top of it before flattening me to his chest.

Now that the sun has dipped below the horizon, we're rendered in complete darkness without the hallway light, and a shudder courses through me. I try to suppress the sobs that quake my body, but the pain in my chest where his words struck burns so furiously that I can hardly stand it.

Flashes of him and Lainey intermingle with his hurtful words, and I try to push him away once more. "Just let me go."

"No," he mumbles, lowering his chin so his face conforms to my neck.

"Beckett, please—"

"I can't let you go," he says more firmly, heating my neck as his lips vibrate against my skin. He breathes deeply, massaging his fingers into the base of my skull with one hand while the other, the arm pressed against my back, grips the material of my shirt. "I'm not mad at you. I'm mad at myself."

The silence builds until I can't take it any longer. I can't stand dancing around how I feel.

Raw and tear-filled, my words slice open the delicate bubble that's held us since we were children.

"How could you let her kiss you?" My voice cracks, and my face is soaked with tears that seep into his shirt. "How could you dance with me like that and then kiss her?"

Beckett slides his hands down my waist, finally allowing me space, but only enough so he can see my face. He searches my eyes, warm hands cupping my cheeks to wipe away the tears. "How can you look at me the way you do and then act like you don't care that she did?"

"Because it *hurt*," I blurt, bowing my neck and placing a palm on his chest. "When I saw her kiss you, it hurt so bad I couldn't breathe. I couldn't think. I felt so— so disposable."

"I feel nothing for her," he exasperates. "The second she kissed me, all I wanted was *you*." He forces me to look at him, pain evident in his voice. "You're all I want. You're all I've ever goddamn wanted; how can't you see that?"

"You chase every vapid, mean girl like it's a sport, and I've spent years dying a little inside every time you meet someone new."

"Why?" he says forcefully. "Tell me why it kills you."

I shake my head and attempt to turn away, but he holds me still.

"*Goddammit*, Mac. Stop running away from me when I'm trying to talk to you. Why—"

"Because I'm in love with you," I erupt, infuriated as the truth strips me bare. Defenseless. "I think I've been in love with you since I was thirteen, and I can't stand it any longer."

Beckett's hands fall to his sides, and I finally break away from him, struggling to think straight through the tension.

I can't believe I said that out loud.

My eyes are downcast as I brace myself for his next words. And despite all he's said, I still fear they're bound to be the rejection I've dreaded since the moment I felt anything for him besides friendship.

"Well, I've got you beat." His rich, breathy voice pierces the silence. "I've been in love with you since I was twelve."

"You—what?" I gape as he moves across the room, and the second the words roll off my lips, they're replaced with his.

Chapter Twelve

WHEN BECKETT'S mouth collides with mine, I'm half convinced it's a dream.

I'm in love with you.

I've been in love with you since I was twelve.

It's as though those voices, those words, belong to two different people. The hands on my waist aren't his, the fingers threaded through his hair aren't mine, and the lips moving together don't belong to either of us.

I grip the front of his shirt for balance, mind spiraling as it catches up with my mouth, registering briefly that I'm kissing Beckett. My best friend in this entire world and the person I've loved more than anyone for so much of my life.

Time slows down as we kiss, and he eventually trails his mouth along my jawline and up my cheek, then simply folds me into his arms. He buries his face in my hair, and my arms lock around his neck, heartbeat pounding against my rib cage.

After a moment, Beckett laughs lightly and pulls away to take me in with his gaze, which travels down my face and over my lips, as though he's seeing me for the first time. His fingers flit across my cheekbones, and he tucks my hair behind my ears.

"What?" I ask, suddenly self-conscious.

Instead of answering, he kisses me again, softer and more deliberate, murmuring against my lips as though he can't believe it's true. "I think that's the first time you've ever yelled at me."

A laugh bubbles in my chest, and his shoulders quake with laughter as his fingers trace the curve of my ear.

"You're really in love with me?" he asks, floored.

I slide my hands over his chest and shoulders, then sweep my thumb over his lower lip.

He sucks in a breath when I nod, and my hands tremble slightly.

"I am," I whisper, unable to believe I'm not only saying it out loud, but that he feels the same. "I love you."

"I love you, too," he breathes, closing his eyes. "When we danced... Mac, that was the first time I ever thought that maybe, just *maybe* you might feel something for me, too. Then Lainey came up to me at the barbecue, and when I told her she was too late, she thought she could change my mind, so she kissed me. I told her I wasn't interested then, and I told her again when she texted me. I was stupid for bringing her up today. I just... I wanted you to tell me not to see her.

When Hannah said you saw it happen... I thought I might've lost you for good."

He pauses, looking so wounded that my chest constricts.

"Then you brushed it off like you couldn't have cared less, and I didn't know what to think or how I'd gotten it so wrong. I thought I'd imagined everything that was happening between us."

"You didn't imagine anything. I pretended I didn't care because I was terrified of how much seeing you with another girl hurt, but the thought of telling you how I felt was even scarier. We've been in each other's lives far too long to throw it all away—I didn't want to lose you."

He presses a kiss to my lips, so sure and confident that my heart melts into a puddle of mush. "I'm going to be in your life one way or another, Mac. You will *always* be my best friend, and nothing could ever change that."

"Are we really doing this?" I whisper.

He hugs me close and rocks me back and forth in his arms. "I don't think we have a choice, do you?"

"No," I admit, knowing that I couldn't live with myself if I didn't explore loving Beckett for real.

His lips find the skin between my throat and collarbone, and he kisses it gently, rubbing his hands over my spine. "Can I ask you something?"

"Anything."

"In all the times I've joked about kissing you... did it ever occur to you that I might be serious?"

I huff out a laugh, embarrassed.

"You said it so often that I thought you were kidding. If you had manned up and kissed me, the message would have been more effective and saved us both a lot of time."

He lifts his head.

"So, in the future..." The dimples in his cheeks deepen with a smile as his lips brush mine. "The direct approach is more effective?"

"Definitely," I confirm, closing my eyes for a moment to let everything sink in.

"Noted." He rubs his thumbs over the corners of my mouth, nodding toward the kitchen. "Are you hungry? I made extra."

"You did?"

He shrugs. "Yeah, I was hoping you wouldn't leave."

"I could eat," I say, and he heads to the counter, flicking on a light above the stove.

In the meantime, I hoist myself onto his bed and feel around for the remote. "Should we watch—"

"No."

I gape, fingers closing around the device. I turn the TV on, squinting against the bright light. "You don't even know what I was going to say."

"You were going to suggest some sappy Nicholas Sparks movie."

"Oh, come on—you love them, and you know it."

Beckett chuckles as he strides across the room with a plate in either hand.

Lifting a knee onto the mattress, he hovers over me and hands me a plate, planting a kiss on my lips. Then another. "I prefer to save the sappy romance for my real life."

I pick up my fork with a smirk, capturing a few noodles and a piece of chicken as Beckett settles beside me. "That was an incredibly charming way of saying you hate my taste in movies."

I stick a forkful of pasta in my mouth, and an explosion of cheeses, garlic, and seasonings blend into the creamiest sauce I've ever tasted.

"Holy crap," I say with my mouth full, savoring every bite. "Becks, this is fantastic. You didn't need my help after all."

Beckett swipes the remote from my thigh with a coy smile. "I can't afford to live off takeout in Boston, so I learned how to cook. I just wanted you here."

Good thing he did. Otherwise, who knows how long it would have taken us to get here if not for the fake proposal.

We finish eating, and Beckett sets our bowls on his nightstand, sliding me so I'm snuggled under his arm. We've watched hundreds of movies together, but we've never watched one like this.

I have no idea what he puts on because I can't focus on anything besides his arms around me, my thighs pressed up against his, and the tranquil billowing of his breath. At a certain point, I stop craning my neck to see the screen and shift farther up so his chin can rest on my head. I pick at a button on his shirt, knuckles grazing his skin.

There's a cluster of half-empty boxes stacked

beneath the kitchen window, and I don't need to look inside to know what they're for.

"When do you go back?" I ask, saddened by the reminder.

"Hhhmm?" He turns the volume down a few notches so he can hear me better.

I point a knuckle toward the boxes, then slide my finger through a buttonhole. "Boston. When do you go back?"

"Eleven days," he says into my hair, sounding tired. "Every one of which we're spending just like this."

I smile, peering up at him. "How do you expect me to serve customers at the diner with my arms around you?"

"You'll find a way," he says confidently. "Besides, I wouldn't mind people seeing you all over me."

This time I full-on laugh. "Is that so?"

"Yep." He places a kiss on the tip of my nose. "Because MacKenzie Roman said she loved me, and I want the whole damn world to know it."

Chapter Thirteen

BECKETT'S DRAPED over my legs, chin resting on my stomach while he waits for me to hang up with Ryan so we can go to breakfast. He slept at my place last night, as opposed to me staying at his like we have the past few days, and we were about to get out of bed right when my brother called.

"Let me know what day you want to fly out, and I can book your flight," Ryan says while simultaneously shushing a crying child in the background.

I purse my lips apprehensively. Sure, he invited me to spend the weekend with him, but I never expected him to pay for my flight. "You don't have to do that. I can scrounge up my tips from the diner and—"

"Don't worry about it. I'm happy to cover the cost," he says, not sounding the least bit concerned about it. Ryan is an attorney and has worked for a really successful firm since he graduated college, so he and Angela live comfortably. Still, I don't want to take advantage of him.

"Would you rather a morn—hold on. Ange? Ange, can you take Emory for five minutes? I can hardly hear myself think."

There's a muffled voice in the background and then the crying fades. "Sorry, it's been a long morning."

"It's fine, but if you're offering me a complimentary vacation, the least I can do is babysit for a night so you and Angela can go out," I insist. From what it sounds like, the two of them haven't had a night out since the kids were born.

"Mac, I can't expect you to do that. You're our guest."

"It's fine, truly. It'll give me a chance to spend more time with the kids." I trap my phone between my ear and shoulder, grabbing Beckett's finger so he'll stop poking my side. He has continuously been trying to get my attention the entire call.

He mouths something unintelligible, and I roll my eyes, asking Ryan to hold on for a second.

Beckett steals the phone from my shoulder and puts it on mute.

"What is with you?" I laugh, and he leans up to brush a kiss on my mouth.

For a second, I think that's all he wanted, but then he pouts, dropping back down and sliding his hands around my waist. "Take me with you."

I blink in surprise. "You want to spend a weekend with my brother's family?"

He nods. "I don't want to spend a weekend away from you so close to me leaving."

I'd intended to visit Ryan *after* Beckett went back to

school so I could spend as much time with him as possible. However, I'm only scheduled to work on Friday this weekend, and it's much easier to ask off one day as opposed to three, which is what I would have to do any other week this month.

Beckett wasn't thrilled when I told him the news, and honestly, I hate that getting to know my brother is infringing on time with my best friend. But I hardly know Ryan, and I won't turn down an opportunity to change that.

"Becks, I can't ask him to do that. He's already paying for my airfare. I can't expect him to put someone else up."

Beckett relents, and although he looks disappointed, I know he understands.

I unmute the call, but the screen doesn't register my touch, so I have to tap it again before bringing the phone back to my ear. "Sorry, about that. I can fly out anytime Friday—whatever's cheapest."

"Okay, let me see what they have available," Ryan says, and I hear his fingers moving rapidly over a keyboard as he checks the available flights.

While I wait, I watch Beckett's eyes droop. We've hardly slept since the other night, having stayed up talking and watching movies until the sun rose.

The line rustles. "All right, check your email to make sure the confirmation came through."

I pull the phone away from my ear and open my emails, brow furrowing.

"I got it, but—"

My brother chuckles, cutting me off. "Next time you mute yourself, make sure you're *actually* muted."

My eyes squeeze shut. "You didn't have to do that."

"Mac, it's fine. Really. Besides, you're marrying him; I want to know your family, too."

I wince. "Thanks, Ryan."

"I'll see you Friday afternoon."

"See you, then."

When we hang up, I can't help the giddy feeling that fills in my chest. Not only am I getting to spend three days with my brother's family, but I won't have to spend them away from Beckett.

I thread my fingers through his hair, gently nudging his head.

He moans, not asleep, but not entirely awake either. "Leave me alone. I'm comfy."

He nuzzles his face in my sweatshirt, tightening his hold on me.

"Becks, I'm hungry," I whine, coaxing him to get up. "Come on."

"If it were up to me, we would have eaten already," he grumbles. "You're the one who had to take a stupid phone call so you can go to stupid Oklahoma without stupid me."

I release an overdramatized sigh, combing his hair with my fingers since it's evident he has no intentions of getting up. "Yeah, you're right. But we could use some time apart anyway."

His head jerks up. "You mean like the *months* we have

to spend without each other while I'm in Boston? That's not enough for you?"

"This will be good practice for then."

Beckett remains unamused. "I don't want practice. I want to spend so much time with you that you beg Boston to take me away."

"Huh," I say thoughtfully. "Then I guess it's a good thing Ryan bought you a ticket."

The smile on his face is immediate. "Are you serious?"

I nod. "He overheard our conversation. You're coming with me."

"Thank God," he exasperates, straightening his arms so he's looming over me. "I've waited for you my whole life. I can't stand the thought of wasting another second before I have to leave."

"Me neither," I tilt my chin up to meet him halfway, heart fluttering as he kisses me.

It's amazing how natural being with him feels— almost like we've been together all these years. Sometimes it seems like we skipped a step, when in reality, we'd been stuck on the same level, never progressing, until now.

I move out of Beckett's grasp after a few seconds, getting off the bed so I can find something to wear. But before I turn away, he locks his arms around my thighs to render me immobile.

"Aren't you the one who was eager to get breakfast?" I ask, peering down at him. "I have to get ready."

He scoots across the mattress so he's in front of me,

grabbing me around the waist instead. "Or we could just make out."

"Now, is that a joke or a hint?" I lean forward, hair dangling on his face.

"A command."

I wrap my fingers around his chin and kiss him long and slow—the kind of kiss that will linger.

I feel him smile as he tugs me onto his lap, but instead of continuing to kiss him, I wrap my arms around his neck in a hug, taking advantage of the strong arms that I know will instantly wrap around me.

If I could go back in time and kiss him all those years ago, when he joked about it for the first time, I wouldn't hesitate.

"I'm glad you're coming with me." My chin rests on his shoulder, and my nose presses against the sleeve of my hoodie.

Beckett places a featherlight kiss on my ear. "Are you worried?"

I nod. I haven't been this nervous about something in a long time. Even when I was afraid Beckett didn't like me back, it was a different kind of anxiety. I always knew he loved me, even if it wasn't in the way I yearned for.

My brother and I went an entire week on vacation barely speaking a full sentence to each other per day. Our relationship has no foundation to fall back on if this doesn't work out. Sure, we've talked on the phone several times since then, but a quick call is different than three days in his *house*.

"They're going to adore you," he assures me.

I'm still not convinced.

This isn't a brief lunch at Panera to start rebuilding a bridge that never existed in the first place. If things get awkward, I can't fake a phone call to leave.

"They will," Beckett says more forcefully.

"How do you know?" I ask, breathing him in. I borrowed his hoodie yesterday and still haven't taken it off. So, between that and sitting on his lap, I'm overwhelmed by the scent of him.

"You're the best person I know. You're gorgeous, funny, considerate, sexy as hell—"

"I don't think my brother is going to take my attractiveness into consideration."

He shrugs innocently. "I got carried away."

I roll my eyes and sit back to look at him.

"My point is, you're an amazing person, and he'd be the *second* luckiest guy in the world to have you in his life." He removes the strands of hair sticking to my cheeks, then places his hands on my hips. "He's your brother, and he wants to get to know you better. Don't overthink it."

"It's hard not to," I admit.

"I know."

"What if I'm not what he expects?" I give life to my worries. "What if after we spend time together, he decides he doesn't want me in his life after all?"

"He won't, I promise," Beckett says with confidence I wish I possessed. "And even if he does, that's just one less person I'll have to fight for your attention."

A surprised laugh escapes me, and I slap his

shoulder, less tense despite the nerves bundled within me. "You're such an asshole."

He chortles before growing serious again. "You have nothing to worry about. I'll be with you every step, okay? You're not doing this alone anymore."

"No, I guess I'm not," I say quietly. A shiver courses through me, and I nestle closer to him.

Truthfully, I've never had to face anything alone because Beckett has always been there, facing it right beside me.

Chapter Fourteen

THE WEATHER in Oklahoma is muggier than I thought possible, and the moment I step foot outside the airport my hair starts to frizz.

I'm only wearing bike shorts and a baggy t-shirt, but the heat is so persistent that I'm tempted to strip off my clothes just so the air can touch my skin.

Beckett and I drag our suitcases past our terminal and toward the short-term parking lot. Angela said it would be easier to find her this way, as opposed to fighting traffic.

She waves when she sees us, hopping out of the car to greet us and wrap me in a hug. She's thirty-one, two years younger than my brother, but doesn't look a day over nineteen—tall and thin, with toned legs accentuated by platform sneakers and skin so perfect it almost looks plastic.

"I'm so glad you could come! Ryan is still at work, but he should be home right around the time we get there," she says, long blonde ponytail swinging when she turns to greet Beckett, pulling him into a hug as well. "You look familiar—were you at our wedding?"

Beckett nods, giving her a dazzling smile. "Yeah, I was Mac's plus one."

"I thought so. You guys were the cutest." She clamps her hands in front of her and gestures to the car. "Should we get on the road? Our house is around forty-five minutes from here, but with traffic, it'll likely take an hour."

We agree, and Beckett opens the passenger door for me before climbing into the back between two booster seats.

"Are the kids still at daycare?" I ask, just to strike up a conversation.

"Yeah, they love it." Angela glances at the sideview mirror before merging lanes and speeding down the exit ramp. "I used to pick them up when I got off work at four, but they would get so mad because all of their friends stayed until six. So now Ryan picks them up so they can stay longer. Eli loves playtime and Emmy adores the arts and crafts."

"That's so sweet," I say, not sure what else to talk about. I truly don't know the first thing about this woman, and subconsciously, I wonder if she's as nervous about making a good impression as I am.

Besides our awkward family vacations, we've never spent any elongated amount of time together. When she married Ryan eight years ago, I had only met her once and it was at her *bridal shower*. Then she held both of her baby showers in Oklahoma, and since my mom had to work, we couldn't go.

Beckett asks her another question about the kids, and I quickly learn that if we ever run out of things to say, the simplest mention of them is enough to get Angela talking for ten minutes straight.

We make ample small talk for the duration of the drive, and she asks basic questions about our relationship and life in Richlynd.

It's not as stressful talking about us now that we're in a real relationship, and I find that I love listening to Beckett talk about our past. Our memories have so many new meanings now that I know he has been in love with me all this time. I find myself rethinking every moment, every joke, every chaste touch with the sole purpose of finding hidden meanings that I overlooked back then.

"When Mac was thirteen, she was asked on a movie date by this douche in my grade—"

"He wasn't a douche," I argue, completely unaware of how we got on this topic. Last I can recall, Beckett was telling her about the annual end-of-summer barbecue, and now somehow, we're reliving one of my top five most embarrassing memories.

"Well, he wasn't me, so he was douche," Beckett amends, and I bury my face in my hands. "Anyway," he continues, undeterred. "She was literally *terrified* that this guy would try to kiss her."

"Okay, *no*. I wasn't terrified he would kiss me. I'd heard about another date he'd been on. They sat in the last row and made out the *entire* movie. I was afraid that's what he was expecting from me."

"Yeah, well, me being the gentleman that I am—I offered to teach her how to kiss. Of course, she turned me down." He shoots me a knowing look, and I snicker, remembering that as the first time he ever teased me about kissing him.

And he wonders why I never thought he was serious —he harassed me with kissing jokes for *weeks* afterward.

"So, did the douche try to kiss you?" Angela asks.

Mortification eats me alive, and Beckett answers before I get the chance. "Nope. *Only* because she made me go into the movie theater first and make the poor kid promise not to."

Angela bursts out laughing, cupping a hand over her mouth as she turns into a long driveway. "I'm assuming there wasn't a second date?"

"No," I grumble, cracking a smile despite my indignation. "But I'd like to highlight that Beckett was more than happy to threaten him."

"Obviously," he retorts. "I didn't want him kissing you any more than you did. Why do you think I waited outside for two hours just to walk you home?"

My lips part, and I'm unable to form a coherent thought as I turn in my seat.

He waited outside?

"I thought you were at the mall with your friends and saw me leaving?"

He shakes his head, cheeks slightly flushed. "I *did* walk around the mall for a little, but I spent most of the night on the bench outside the movie theater. I was afraid if the date went well, you'd change your mind and let him kiss you goodnight. I didn't want to give him the chance."

I blink in astonishment, thinking back on that night. Sure enough, the moment I stepped outside with my date, Beckett was there offering to walk me home.

But then I dig a little deeper.

"Oh my God—Aiden Fisher, eighth grade," I say, suspecting he'll know exactly what I'm talking about.

Angela pulls the car into the garage, and I open my door, waiting for Beckett to validate my claim while he gets our luggage from the back.

When he still doesn't answer, I walk around the car. "Beckett Harlow, what did you do?"

He winces. "I *might* have insinuated that I'd knock his teeth out if I ever caught him kissing you again."

Well, that would explain why, after a month of dating, he started treating me like I had the plague. He wouldn't even let me borrow a pencil in class when I asked. I got written up for "not being prepared" on a test day thanks to him.

Gritting my teeth, I close my fist around the handle of my suitcase, leveling with him.

"James Lewis flirted with me all night at homecoming and then never spoke to me again."

"Yeah. Guilty."

"Beckett."

"You were supposed to be hanging out with me," he

reasons, and the wounded innocence on his face makes it hard to be mad.

"What about Tony?" I ask. "We dated for over a year, and you didn't bother to scare him off."

Beckett fidgets with the handle of his bag as Angela closes the hatchback, appearing amused by our banter. "By that time, I was in Boston and had started to give up on us. He was a decent guy, so I figured if I couldn't have you, then you should be with someone like him."

Of *all* the guys, he left Tony Jenkins alone. The one man who, at the time, I wouldn't have minded missing out on.

Though, I expect that's exactly why Beckett let him be. Tony was never a threat because he knew we'd never last.

When Beckett dated other girls, I was always incredibly jealous, but I never stepped outside of the best friend's role. Beckett did. Repeatedly. And I had no idea.

While Angela heads toward the door that leads into the house, I hold Beckett back. I touch a hand to his torso and rise on my toes to kiss his cheek. His abdominal muscles flex beneath my fingers as they slide over his shirt.

"What was that for?" he asks, eyebrows drawing together in bewilderment.

Some girls might be appalled that he sabotaged my chances with every guy who showed interest in me, but in reality, *he* was the only guy I was wholeheartedly interested in. I've never known true heartbreak because no one who held my heart had the power over it that he does.

"Just because," I say, then turn to follow Angela.

There's a short hallway on the other side of the door with a view straight into the kitchen. The room is gorgeous—modern with white marble floors and a black and white backsplash. High ceilings dome at the center of the room, an archway separating it from what appears to be a large dining room. Everything about this place is *classy,* and it fits my brother well.

"You got here faster than I anticipated," Ryan says, appearing in the archway with Emory on his hip. He's still in his work clothes—a well-fitted gray suit with a navy blue tie. His face is clean-shaven, and his hair is slicked back so finely that there isn't a strand out of place.

He bends to kiss Angela, and she stretches to meet him, removing their youngest from his arms at the same time. "We didn't hit much traffic."

Angela bops Emory's nose, and she giggles vehemently.

"I'm happy you guys are here," Ryan says, giving me a hug. "Beckett, it's good to see you again."

"You, too." Beckett steps forward to shake his hand, then gestures around us. "This place is gorgeous."

"Thank you. We just had it remodeled, actually. Ange, will you keep an eye on the kids while I show them to their rooms? Eli's in the playroom."

Angela nods, and Ryan motions for us to follow him through several expansive rooms until we reach a stairway. It ascends to a modest sitting room with a pure white carpet and brown leather couches situated to face a flatscreen on the wall straight ahead. Parallel to it on either side are hallways that lead to what appear to be the guest rooms.

There's a full bathroom right off the sitting area that we'll have to share, but otherwise, we have our own rooms and an entire floor to ourselves.

"Make yourselves at home. We're just up the stairwell on the other side of the house, so if you need anything at any hour, don't hesitate to let us know. I'm going to help Angela start dinner—" He holds up a hand the second I open my mouth, "—you're our guests, you're not helping. Four hours is a long time to sit on a plane, so get settled in, relax if you want to. Dinner should be ready around seven. If you want, you can even take a walk around the neighborhood or check out the community lake. There's around ten acres on either side of each residence, so we have plenty of privacy."

I glance at Beckett, and he shrugs, not caring what we do.

"We'll probably unpack first, and I might shower before dinner," I say. Between the flight, a forty-five-minute layover, and the Oklahoma humidity, I feel like I haven't had a proper cleanse in days.

"No problem. There are fresh towels under the sink." Ryan starts to back out of the room but pauses in the doorway. "Oh, and I meant to congratulate you guys on your engagement. If you need any ideas for the wedding, Angela has a *detailed* itinerary from ours—she was an event coordinator for a local hotel before we got married."

"I'll keep that in mind... thanks, Ryan." I force a smile.

Beckett rolls his suitcase into his room, then does the same with mine while I check out the bathroom. It's *huge*, and the tile shower has a magnetic glass door.

"Mac, they put *mints* on our pillows." Beckett whistles, keeping his voice low since there isn't a door separating the sitting room from the downstairs. I doubt they can hear us from the kitchen, but still. He comes up behind me, wrapping his arms around my waist and kissing my neck. "I freaking love your family."

His breath smells like mint, and I stare at him through the mirror. "You ate mine, too, didn't you?"

"Why, did you want some?" he teases, bowing his neck to meet my lips. My eyes flutter closed as I tilt my chin up, body inclining into his as the sultry taste of mint and rich dark chocolate tantalizes my tongue.

Warmth spreads across my chest, and I reach over my shoulder to graze the light stubble on his cheek.

His palm drifts across my stomach, and he inhales, kissing me twice before resting the side of his head against mine.

A tiny smirk tugs at his lips, and he holds up a piece of chocolate, wrapped neatly in green foil.

My mouth falls open. "You tricked me."

He chuckles as I unwrap the square, placing it on the center of my tongue and closing my eyes to fully experience the slow melt.

Beckett simply holds me, occasionally kissing my temple or my cheek as though to remind himself that he can after so much wasted time. I lift my gaze to take in his reflection; arms around my waist, head pressed to mine, soft eyes trailing over my profile.

Knowing what it's like to kiss him, to be curled in the comfort of his arms, I can't fathom how I ever denied him.

"No one will ever believe we called off our engagement with you looking at me like that," he whispers, gently swaying us side to side.

My heart thuds in my chest at the reminder of our lie, and I want more than anything to forget it ever happened.

We have to tell people something—our families, at the very least. But how do you explain to your loved ones that you seized an opportunity to fake an engagement with your best friend, fell in love with each other in the process, and now want to *call off* the engagement but continue dating? Because we can't very well "break up" and then sneak around to avoid explaining ourselves. That's no better than what we're doing now.

"Our three weeks aren't up yet," I reason, sliding my fingers over the grooves in his knuckles. "We still have time to figure out how to handle it."

"Not here," he whispers, and there's a sudden distance in his expression. "This trip is about you and your brother's family. We'll worry about us when we get home."

"Before you leave for Boston," I clarify, for no reason

other than to vocalize my discontentment with his departure.

"It won't change a thing," he says, breath warming the side of my cheek. "It never has before. You'll still be the first person I want to see in the morning and the last before I fall asleep at night."

I nod, rotating so I'm facing him. "I know. I just hate the idea of missing you every day."

It's always hard when he leaves, but this year, the loss feels greater.

"Me, too." His hands knead my waist, and his blue eyes search mine solemnly. "We'll make it work." He tucks my hair behind my ears, pressing a light kiss on my nose. "With as long as we've waited to be right here, a few months apart won't mean a thing." He dips his chin, lips capturing mine as he whispers more assurances. "We'll be okay."

He's right. This is nothing we haven't faced before. Besides, if I spend the entire weekend concerned with our engagement and Boston, then what was the purpose of this trip?

I don't know how he always manages to break through the sea of doubts in my mind and calm the rushing waters, but he does. Every single time.

Chapter Fifteen

WATER TRICKLES down the sides of my thigh, and I peek over my sunglasses to see Eli dunk his head underwater, only to bob up a few feet away. He looks around innocently, and I smile, closing my eyes again. My fingers dip into the tepid lake, stirring in small circles as I settle deeper into my raft.

We spent the morning in the city, where Angela and Ryan took us for breakfast and showed us around a bit. Then we drove back to their house and decided to relax at the lake on the edge of their property.

The area is beautifully rural. Quiet. I love the vacant roads and absence of the small-town bustle I've gotten used to in Richlynd. Their neighborhood is secluded, and if you're not paying attention when you pass the entrance, you could easily miss it.

Eli emerges beside my raft again, and I peer through squinted eyes as he cups lake water in his small hands, allowing it to drip between his fingers and onto my thigh. Meanwhile, Emmy is on the bank, picking flowers and arranging them in the grass around her. Eli was helping her for a while, but he must have gotten bored since he's resorted to ninja-ing around me. He's a lot shyer than his sister, who's surprisingly direct for a four-year-old.

"Eli, let MacKenzie be," Ryan says.

"Dad," he whines, throwing his head back as though everything is ruined now.

I sit up abruptly, gaping at my nephew. "That was *you* putting water in my raft? I thought I was losing my mind."

He cackles with a toothy grin, pressing his fingers into his chin. "No, it was me, see!"

Eli then proceeds to show me how he'd been sneaking around, and I pretend to be shocked, which makes him incredibly happy.

Ryan calls the kids to get lunch, opening the cooler he packed while the rest of us loaded the rafts, towels, and folding chairs onto a four-wheeler.

"I bet I can swim faster," Eli announces.

Beckett, who has been floating on his own raft, takes that as a challenge. "You're on. Winner gets the sandwich with extra turkey."

"Deal." He beams. "Ready, set, go!"

The three of us dive into the water, Beckett and me intentionally lagging to give him a better chance. The water ripples over my skin as I tread, gradually catching up with Eli so he doesn't think we let him win. Though, that kid is *fast*. I'm not sure either of us could have beat him if we tried.

"You guys are *slow*," he remarks, shaking his hair out and jogging toward Ryan. "I won, so I get the sandwich with extra turkey on it."

Ryan chuckles. "Okay, buddy."

Eli takes his lunch and happily skips over to Emory, who's eating a PB&J surrounded by her flower collection.

"They love you," Ryan remarks as I wiggle a pair of jean shorts over my bathing suit bottoms.

"We love them," I counter and sit on the grass beside his chair, taking a sandwich and biting into the turkey and mayo concoction.

Beckett agrees as he wrings the water out of his swim trunks, then does the same, settling beside me so his knee touches mine.

We eat in silence until Ryan speaks up. "How does your mom feel about you coming here?"

I finish chewing, taking my time as I swallow and take a sip of the lemonade Angela made. She ran back to the house for more bottled water and to make a reservation for dinner tonight, since Beckett and I insisted they go out.

"She was surprised," I admit. Though, I don't miss how he refers to her as *my* mom. Their relationship was always rocky, especially after he left. But marrying Angela without so much as introducing her to us first was the last straw. My dad doesn't care quite so much, and I'm almost certain he talks to Ryan more than my mom realizes. Family vacations are her only way of keeping the grandkids in her life. "To be honest, I think she was a little jealous."

He rolls his eyes, peering over his shoulder to watch Angela walk toward us. "I'm not the one who burned that bridge. She couldn't get over herself long enough to give Angela a chance. I'd already wanted out; she just shoved me the rest of the way."

I nod, knowing all of this already.

"You're lucky, you know," he says, jutting his chin toward Beckett. "You met the perfect person for you *and* her. I'm sure she was ecstatic when she heard the news."

My eyes roll back in my head, and I pick at a piece of crust. "You could say she's been waiting for me to meet someone special for a while."

And as the words leave my mouth, I suddenly understand why. She wants a do-over. To amend the mistakes she made with Ryan. She's known Beckett all our lives, loves his family, and doesn't have to worry about any surprises. He's the polar opposite of Angela.

"I never asked how you proposed." Angela directs her question toward Beckett, setting another cooler filled with bottled water behind us.

"It was at the mall," he says, teeth capturing his lip before he takes the last bite of his sandwich.

"The mall?" she asks. "That must be quite a story."

He clears his throat, wiping crumbs off his hands. "Not really. We were shopping for my parents' anniversary gift, and I just... dropped to a knee. Now here we are."

"Ryan, how did you propose?" I change the subject,

placing a hand on Beckett's thigh. He rubs his hand over mine as my brother starts telling us about the romantic evening he planned for Angela.

I'm only half listening, though.

We're supposed to be finding our footing in each other's lives, not starting our relationship off with a lie. But the thing about lies is, once you're in so deep, it becomes harder to find your way out.

Angela is upstairs washing the lake grime off the kids before she gets ready, and in the meantime, Ryan orders pizza for us from the other room.

Beckett and I took turns showering, and now we're sitting in the kitchen, waiting for Angela and Ryan to leave. My arms and chest are pink from the sun, meanwhile, Beckett's tan skin is a half shade darker.

"Are you absolutely sure—"

"We're happy to watch the kids," Beckett says, looking up as Angela appears, wearing a flowy green dress and sandals. She has asked us that question more times than I can count in the past few hours.

She nods. "I know, I know. But you just spent the whole day with them, I'd hate for you to feel forced to babysit."

"It's no problem at all," I assure her. "Besides, you two deserve a night out."

If anything, being with the kids today has motivated me to spend more time with them. Not to mention, this is the least we can do when they've paid our way this entire visit. Ryan has refused to let us spend a dime since we got here. He wouldn't even let me pay for sunscreen at a convenience store when I realized I had forgotten mine at home.

"Are you sure *you* wouldn't rather have a nice dinner alone somewhere? It's your first trip as an engaged couple, you should be celebrating."

I stand, taking her hands seriously. I think she truly believes that going out and enjoying herself is neglecting her parental duties and burdening us in some way. "Ange, we're thrilled to watch the kids. Beckett and I have spent just about every moment together since we were kids. Meanwhile, I've missed out on *years* of my niece and nephew's lives. I'll take all the time I can get with them this weekend."

Angela sighs, and it seems I've rebutted every single one of her arguments. She pulls me into a hug and moves to Beckett next, vanilla perfume lingering in the air even after she backs away. "You two are saints."

"You ready?" Ryan asks, and then after a dozen more 'thank yous' and a few quick reminders about the kids, Beckett and I manage to shove them out the door.

He turns the lock behind them, and we head toward the playroom, where Eli is curled up on the couch with toy soldiers littered on the cushions and floor around him, eyes opening and closing slowly. Angela said the lake probably tired him out, so our job should be pretty easy.

Emmy, on the other hand, is sitting at a table behind

the couch. It's right in front of glass doors that overlook the lake, and you can just see the water over the trees, lit by the moonlight.

The moment she sees us, she jumps up and grabs our hands, leading us to the table and sitting us on either side of her. She pushes a piece of paper at each of us, then taps the box of crayons in the middle of the table.

"Be careful. Mommy gets mad if you color on the table." Her pudgy finger traces at a few red and blue lines on the wood where she must have accidentally colored off the paper.

Beckett laughs and grabs some crayons. "We'll be very careful."

"Do you make bracelets?" I ask, noticing a Rainbow Loom kit next to Emmy's seat. Her face lights up and she nods eagerly, abandoning a picture of what vaguely resembles the sky. She sets the plastic case on the table, and when Beckett puts his crayon down to watch us, she picks it up and thrusts it back in his hand.

"Keep drawing."

"You heard her," I sass, and Beckett shakes his head. "Only the girls get to make bracelets."

Eli appears beside me and stands on his tiptoes to see above the table, grabbing onto my wrist for leverage. "Can I make one?"

Emmy refuses, and he pouts. When it looks like he might burst into tears, I turn in my seat and stroke the light brown hair off his forehead. "I think Beckett needs help with his picture. He's not very good at drawing."

"I know how to draw," Eli says hopefully.

He hops toward the chair beside Beckett and climbs onto it, using the wooden bars on the back to hoist him to his knees. He scoots the chair closer, and Beckett puts the piece of paper between them.

While the two of them get to work, discussing who should draw what, Emmy sets the plastic loom in front of me and dumps a bag of pink and white rubber bands on the table.

"I can set it up," she says, then chews her lip in deep concentration while she stretches the rubber bands over each peg, overlapping them in a way that they'll loop together when we start the bracelet.

"I'm pretty bad," she informs me, gesturing toward a bag full of bracelets that are falling apart.

"I can teach you if you want. I used to make these when I was a kid."

"Really?" she asks eagerly.

"All the time." Honestly, I had no idea kids still played with Rainbow Loom at all.

She smiles to herself as she finishes laying the groundwork for the bracelet. Then, to my surprise, she pulls out another loom, sliding the first one to me. "Can we make them match?"

"I'd love that."

We take a quick break when the pizza is delivered, and then, step by step, I show her how to make a bracelet. By the time we're done, she can hardly sit still in her chair.

"It worked! It didn't fall apart!" She jumps off her

FALL FOR ME

chair, practically launching herself onto my lap and hooking her arms around my neck. "Thanks, Aunt Mac!"

She then grabs her bracelet and hops off my lap to show Beckett.

"Becky!" she says, which is what she has resorted to calling him because she can't quite remember the "ett" part of his name.

She loops her arm around his elbow and climbs onto his chair next, so he has no choice but to abandon his and Eli's drawing. "Look what Aunt Mac helped me make!"

Beckett examines the bracelet, looking impressed. "Wow, Emmy. That looks *so* good."

She sits on his lap, facing the table and leaning against his stomach. "What are you drawing."

"Us at the lake today." Eli sits up, looking sad all of a sudden.

I think he gets a little jealous of Emmy sometimes. He's social in an indirect way—like at the lake today— whereas Emory is very forward.

Noticing the change in Eli's demeanor, Beckett holds out his arm and scoops Eli into his lap, balancing both kids on his knees. Eli points to each of the stick figures standing around a blue circle, which I'm assuming is in representation of the lake. "That's Mommy and Daddy in the water. And there's us, running from Aunt Mac and Uncle Beckett. See—everyone's smiling!"

"What's in my hair?" I ask, tapping the orange polka dots drawn on my head.

189

Beckett huffs a laugh and Eli giggles. It seems they're in on some kind of joke together.

"Beckett was s'posed to put the flowers Emmy picked in your hair, but he's not very good. You were right."

Beckett tickles Eli's stomach, and he giggles madly. He clutches Beckett's fingers with his tiny hands, which barely wrap around one of them.

"Emmy, will you make me a bracelet?" Beckett asks, and she nods, all business.

Instead of going back to her seat, though, she presses her belly to the table so she can reach across it and grab her loom. Then, upon realizing all the bands are pink, she hops off and grabs a different color before returning to her seat on Beckett's lap.

"I'll make yours blue because you're a boy," she says matter-of-factly.

"Can you make me one, too?" Eli asks, and it takes me a moment to realize he's talking to me.

I check the time. Angela said she usually puts them to bed at eight, but not to worry too much about it. It's already eight-thirty, but I agree anyway. I don't think any amount of warm milk will get these two to sleep right now.

"Fine, but we have to put you to bed by nine at the latest, okay?"

They ignore that last part, not the least bit concerned about missing their bedtime.

Eli slides down Beckett's knee and comes to sit on my lap instead. He watches me twist and fold the rubber bands around each other, and much to Emmy's dismay, I let him do some of them himself.

Once we're finished, Emmy sleepily puts her bracelet around Beckett's wrist, and I put mine on Eli.

"We have to add them to the picture," he announces, reaching for his drawing.

Once he adds blue lines to his and Beckett's wrists, and pink lines to mine and Emmy's, we carry the kids upstairs to their bedroom, which is right beside Angela and Ryan's.

We put them in their PJs, and despite Emmy's exhaustion, sleep is the last thing on her mind.

She forces us to lie on the floor, then grabs a remote off Eli's bed. She clicks a button that shuts off the lights and turns on a projector that displays stars all over the ceiling. Beckett rolls his head to the side, grinning at me as Emmy curls up between us in the crook of my arm. Eli does the same with Beckett, and the four of us watch the stars swirl around the ceiling in a dim blue light.

Eli and Emmy fall asleep almost immediately, and Beckett dozes off soon after, leaving me to watch the stars alone.

A little while later, two shadows appear in the doorway, and I crane my neck to find my brother and his wife smiling down at us.

Angela puts a finger to her lips and moves into the room, scooping Emmy off the floor. She hardly stirs as she's placed in her twin bed. Ryan grabs Eli and does the same while I lightly shake Beckett's shoulder.

His brows scrunch slightly before he looks around the room groggily.

"Where are we?" he mumbles, rubbing his eyes as he attempts to get his bearings.

"You fell asleep in the kids' room," I whisper, taking his hand and pulling him to his feet.

We quietly say goodnight to Angela and Ryan in the hallway, and then I lead Beckett down the stairs, through several rooms, and then up the stairs to our rooms. He tries to collapse on the couch in the sitting area, but I guide him away from it, down the hall, and to his room.

Half out of it, he stumbles into bed without turning on the lights and struggles to remove his t-shirt. I help him pull it over his head, then set it on his suitcase, but as I turn to leave, his hand closes around my wrist. He tugs me onto the mattress, lifting the sheets and pulling me flat against him.

"Stay," he murmurs with a sleepy kiss, snaking his arms around my waist and resting his head against my chest.

I shift farther down the bed so I can share his pillow, shivering when the air conditioner kicks on. Beckett maneuvers the sheet over my exposed shoulder, and I place a gentle kiss on his lips. He smiles, still out of it, and I doze off soon after he does, tangled in his arms.

Chapter Sixteen

SUN BEAMS through the sheer gray curtains of the guest room, and I grunt my disapproval of its brightness, tucking my chin under the covers to shield my eyes. My back is snug against Beckett's chest and my legs are curled into me, but as hard as I try, can't fall back to sleep.

Beckett's palm slides across my stomach, and I feel his chest rise behind me, so I roll over, shifting my sweater when it tangles around my thighs. His eyes are still closed, but he kisses my forehead and snuggles me closer. I trail my fingers over his biceps and down to the crook of his elbow, watching as his eyelashes flutter and lift to reveal his pure blue eyes. The sun glints off his smooth skin, and his mouth curves subtly when he takes me in.

"Morning," he says, voice deep and gritty.

"Morning," I repeat, rubbing the sleep from my eyes.

He groans, bowing his head and burying his face in the crook of my neck. "What time is our flight again?"

"Not until two," I respond, weaving my fingers through his hair. "We should probably pack before breakfast so we don't have to later."

He doesn't make a move to get up. "Mmhmm."

We lie here for a little while longer, and then Beckett peppers light kisses along my collarbone before he rolls away, dragging his fingers down my forearm and placing a kiss on my inner wrist next.

His absence bathes me in cold air, and I fold my arms against my chest, shuddering. I watch him stride across the room to his suitcase, where he slides his arms through a teal button-down, not bothering to fold his clothes as he shoves the rest of them inside.

I snicker, and he shoots me a dark look over his shoulder.

"They need to be washed anyway. Who cares if they're wrinkled?"

Rolling my eyes, I throw the covers off and place my bare feet on the white carpet. "You will when you get to your last few shirts and can't fit them inside. Move."

I shove him out of the way and scoop up the shirts he haphazardly crumpled into his small suitcase.

"I'll do this. Do you think you can manage packing the toiletries?"

"Yes, *Mom,*" he grumbles in my ear, lips brushing my temple as he passes.

I shake my head with a smile, carefully folding each of his dirty shirts. Then I refold the two he didn't wear just for the hell of it, fluffing a cream sweatshirt that was rolled into a ball. My eyes catch on the red lettering embroidered on the front with his school's logo.

Freaking Boston.

I never thought I could hate a place I'd never visited so much, but I don't have much of a choice when it's constantly taking him away from me.

With a heavy heart, I fold the remainder of his clothes and zip the suitcase. Then I strip his bed and throw the sheets in the hamper before remaking it with clean ones.

Beckett appears in the doorway a few minutes later, toiletry bag in hand. He looks around with wide eyes. "You did all of this in the time it took me to pack our soap?"

I snort, slipping past him. "Well, if I left it up to you, we'd miss our flight."

He laughs as I head to my room to change, throwing on a fitted t-shirt and jeans. Then I pack my things and head to the bathroom, where Beckett was smart enough to leave out the necessities so I could brush my teeth and put on a little makeup.

He's waiting for me in the sitting room when I emerge with freshly brushed teeth and a coat of mascara, and then we follow the scent of bacon and syrup to the kitchen.

Emmy and Eli are sitting at the table, digging their forks into two small stacks of pancakes. Emmy grins when she sees us, food hanging out of her mouth. "Did you like the stars?"

"Finish chewing, please," Angela says, carrying a plate full of pancakes to the table. She then grabs a napkin to wipe up the crumbs that Emmy spit, along with the syrup crusted in the corners of her mouth. "It's not polite to talk with your mouth full."

Emmy chews and swallows quickly, then repeats her question. I assume she's asking if we liked the projector in their room last night.

"The stars were beautiful," I tell her, leaning to place a kiss on the top of her head. She swings her legs under the table with a happy smile. I walk around the table to place a kiss on Eli's head next. "Good morning, Eli."

"'Morning, Aunt Mac," he beams. Beckett ruffles his hair, which only makes his smile grow wider.

"They can't stop gushing about last night," Angela says, looking rather happy herself. "You guys made quite the impression. They keep asking if you're going to live with us permanently."

Beckett and I laugh, taking two seats between the kids. Beckett uses the spatula to pile a few pancakes on my plate before serving himself.

"I wish. It's so peaceful here. You guys are in your own little world," I say, drizzling syrup on my plate before handing it to Beckett, who douses his pancakes.

"Yes, it's quite different from where you live," Angela agrees. "I think the kids missed out growing up without you in their lives. I'm an only child, and my parents, their only family, live in Texas, so we don't see them as often as we'd like. Having you here was really nice. For all of us."

"For us, too," I say, bringing a forkful to my mouth.

"We need to make it a point to talk more. And if you and Ryan ever want to pawn the kids off for a weekend getaway, I'd be more than happy to watch them."

I could swear Angela's eyes moisten, but she blinks the tears away and moves around the table to pull me into a one-armed hug.

"You're too kind, Mac. Thank you." She clears her throat, then gestures to a closed door off the kitchen. "Ryan has a few business calls to make this morning, but once he's done, he'll drive you to the airport around noon."

I nod somberly, just as sad about leaving here as I am Beckett heading to Boston in a few days.

Mirroring my thoughts, Emmy sets her fork down, eyes clouding over. "You're *leaving?*"

Angela strokes her cheek lovingly. "Yeah, sweetie, they have to go back home. Though, I'm sure we can convince Aunt Mac to video chat with you and Eli sometime."

"No convincing necessary," I say, reaching to take her little hand in mine. "I will call you every week. I promise."

This earns me a teary-eyed smile, and Emmy sniffles, wiping a fist under her nose and eyes before going back to her pancakes.

"You promise?" Eli asks, and the worry written on that poor boy's face splits my heart in two.

"Yeah, buddy, I promise."

We finish our breakfast and carry our suitcases to the front door, then head back to the table. We talk with

Angela and the kids for a while, and when it's time to go, Emmy and Eli run to the living room and return with our bracelets and the picture Beckett helped draw.

"Promise to wear them every day," Emmy says, pressing the bracelets to her lips, doe eyes hopeful.

"I promise," Beckett says, scooping her and Eli into a group hug.

Emmy turns to me next. "Promise?"

I hold a pinky out to both of them, and they hook theirs around it. "Promise."

I wrap their tiny bodies in my arms and squeeze the life out of them. "I'll talk to you guys soon, okay?"

They nod simultaneously, clutching Angela's legs while Beckett and I take turns hugging her goodbye.

"Thanks again for having me and extending an invitation to Beckett."

"Your family is our family, Mac." She places a hand on my cheek and tucks a strand of hair behind my ear. "You two be safe, and good luck at school, Beckett."

"Bye, Ange," I hug her one last time.

Beckett rolls our luggage to the garage, and we pack it in the cargo area while we wait for Ryan to finish up his last call of the morning. He took yesterday off and asked to work from home today so he could drive us to the airport, but he still has responsibilities to his clients. Being a lawyer means he's never really off the clock.

When he's finally ready, we get in the car, and as we're pulling out of the garage, I wave to Angela and the kids, who are standing at the front door to see us off.

We make small talk during the drive, but the closer we get to the airport, the more depressed I become.

"I'm really glad we got to do this," Ryan says as he parks outside our terminal. He hops out of the car to get our suitcases, then wraps me in a hug. "If you ever feel the urge to visit again, just let me know. You're welcome anytime."

"Next weekend then?" I joke, chest feeling tight. He truly made us feel like part of the family this weekend.

He chuckles, placing a hand on the back of my head. "The plane ticket is on me."

I bite my lip to hold back the tears threatening to fall. "Thanks, Ryan. For everything."

He releases me to shake Beckett's hand, and the two exchange goodbyes while I stare at our luggage sadly.

Then we watch him drive away, and an empty weight presses down on my chest.

I step into Beckett's arms, and he holds me tight, resting his chin atop my head.

"I wish they didn't live so far," I whisper, melting against him.

His hands rub my back. "I know."

"And now we either have to suffer through this stupid engagement dinner tomorrow or come clean about everything," I whisper, gripping the back of his shirt.

And you're leaving.

I shut my eyes and tighten my hold on his waist, trying not to linger on the thought that the next time I'm outside an airport, it will be to see him off.

After two flights and a layover in Denver, we arrive home around seven-thirty. I fell asleep on the last flight, utterly exhausted from travel, being sad about leaving Oklahoma, and the anticipation of saying goodbye to Beckett next.

"I'm going to drop my stuff off and tell my parents we're home, then we can head to your place," Beckett says, turning into his parents' driveway.

It's hazy out, and the sound of crickets seeps through the open windows as he turns the ignition off. He hops out of the car, and I follow, figuring I'll say hello to his parents while I'm here.

I wait outside while he carries his suitcase to his apartment, then we cut across the yard toward the patio, where his parents are likely eating dinner in the sunroom.

"Hey," I begin, stopping him before we reach the door and our vacation officially ends. I rise on my feet and draw him close, kissing him long and slow. He cups my face in his hands and tilts his head on an inhale. I run my hands over his chest, savoring every breath and stroke of his tongue, and then eventually I break away. His ragged breath covers the lower half of my face, and when I speak, my mouth touches his. "I'm really glad you came."

He ducks his chin to kiss the corner of my jaw before collecting me in his embrace. "I am, too."

My chest expands. "I love you."

"I love you, too."

Reluctantly, we separate, and he tries the back door. It's unlocked, so we head inside, and he calls out for his parents.

"Anyone home?"

There's no answer, so we walk through the kitchen and dining room, stopping at the living room, where both of our families are sitting around the couch.

There's a bottle of wine and four empty glasses on the coffee table, and the dimmed lights shadow their faces as we walk around the couch.

"What are you guys doing here?" I ask, crossing my arms and leaning into Beckett's side.

"I don't know," Mom says, looking between us with an unreadable expression. "Is there anything you'd like to tell us?"

I swallow, clearing my throat. "I'm... not sure what you mean."

"How about you explain to me why, when I called the jeweler you told me about to check on the progress of your ring, they said they'd never heard of you." Her eyes drag to Beckett, lips in a tight line. "*Either* of you. Not first names, not last names. They didn't even have a record of anyone purchasing or requesting a resize the day you got engaged."

Beckett exhales beside me, cracking a nervous smile. "Jeweler-consumer confidentiality...?"

Mrs. Harlow closes her eyes, and both of our dads exchange weary glances. Meanwhile, my mother shoots daggers at him with her eyes.

I suck on my teeth, slightly perturbed. "You *called* the jeweler?"

"That is not the point."

"Isn't it, though?" I ask. "It's not your wedding. You had no business—"

"Forgive me, but it doesn't appear to be your wedding either," she says, raising a firm hand to silence me.

Beckett squeezes my hip, and I refrain from responding.

Mrs. Harlow rises from her seat, palms pressed together in front of her with ill-contained fury. "Are you or are you not engaged?"

"We're not," Beckett says.

"Then why on Heaven's Earth would you pretend to be?" she shouts, and I don't think I've ever heard his mom raise her voice before.

Beckett winces, pinching the bridge of his nose. "It was all a huge misunderstanding. Someone misinterpreted a joke for a proposal, and we went along with it. Then..." He looks down at me. "Then things got complicated."

"So, this was all some sick joke?" his dad asks, looking incredibly disappointed. "Were you ever planning to tell us the truth?"

"Yes, of course," I say, not entirely sure what we would have done. "We were always going to call it off before Beckett left."

My mom's frown deepens. "MacKenzie, I cannot believe you would do something like this."

"If you hadn't put so much pressure on me to meet a

man, or threatened to force Tony on me again, I never would have felt like I had to," I reason, though throwing blame probably isn't the best idea. "Yes, I lied, and I'm sorry, but I wouldn't have agreed to this if you had left me alone."

"This whole thing was *your* idea," she turns on Beckett, and it seems that's all she took from my monologue—that I *agreed* to this.

"No—" I start, but Beckett slides his hand across my back, stopping me.

"It's okay, Mac. It was my idea."

"We both agreed. I could have said no, but I didn't want to."

My mom stands from the couch, fuming. "Does your brother know you're a fraud? Is that why you wanted to spend the weekend with him?"

"Nicole," my dad says in a warning tone. "Enough."

She bites her tongue, glancing at the Harlows. "We'll finish this at home. Thank you for the wine. Mac, let's go."

She and my dad head toward the door, but Beckett grabs my hand before I can walk away. "Want me to come over later?"

"No, this might take a while." I kiss his cheek. "I'll come back when things simmer down."

"Okay." He strokes my face and then presses a kiss on my lips even though both of our parents are likely watching. "I'm sorry."

My gaze drifts from his eyes to his lips and back again. "Me, too."

I avoid his parents' gazes as I pass, too embarrassed by our lie.

"So, you faked an engagement, but you're *actually* together?" his mom asks, sounding incredibly confused.

"I love her," I hear him say as I step out the door. I glance back to find him watching me. "Always have."

"*MacKenzie*," my mom scolds, standing outside my car. I assume they walked here since theirs is nowhere in sight, but there's no way in hell I'm subjecting myself to an enclosed space with my mother this enraged.

"I'm walking," I holler over my shoulder, passing the garage and starting toward our house through the grassy field.

Much to my dismay, they follow behind me, and just as well, I'm almost positive Beckett pocketed my keys when we got out of the Jeep earlier.

"Why don't we all cool off and talk about this later," Dad says, looking around. The last thing he probably wants is for the whole neighborhood to hear Mom screaming at me.

"How can you be so calm about this?" she spats. "She has been lying to us for weeks. First Ryan married some woman we didn't know existed, and now Mac faked being in love with the boy we've known since they were kids."

I grit my teeth. "I didn't fake being in love with him, and I'm not your do-over for Ryan."

"I beg your pardon?"

"You didn't have a say in his life from the moment he turned eighteen, and ever since, you've been trying to subtly orchestrate mine. Why else call about the ring? Force an engagement dinner on us when I told you we weren't ready to celebrate?"

"Because *normal* couples want to celebrate with their families," she says. "How were you planning to undo this? Don't you understand how this reflects on both of you if people find out?"

I reach our driveway, stomping up the front porch and into the house. "We were going to tell everyone we're better as friends, but halfway through, we realized we were never *just friends* to begin with. We'd always planned to call it off after he went back to school, but we weren't sure how to do it now that we're together."

"Well, we need to figure something out because—"

"I don't want to tell anyone yet," I interrupt. "You guys know and that's all that matters. Beckett and I will decide when and how we want to deal with this."

She closes her eyes, dark circles more prominent tonight than usual. "You want *us* to lie for you? You think—"

"I've been doing it for weeks. Just keep your answers vague," my dad interrupts, and her nostrils flare.

"You knew?"

"I found out the afternoon of the barbecue."

"I swear to God," she grits, clenching her fists. "Both of our kids got the worst sides of themselves from you."

I scoff. "It's not *his* ugly side that's showing right now."

An argument spawns between my parents, and I turn

on my heels, climbing the stairs and shutting my bedroom door quietly.

I drop my head in my hands, combatting a headache, and it's not until I lift it that I realize, not only is my luggage still in my car at Beckett's house, but so is my phone.

I wait until the yelling dies down and a door slams, then I sneak downstairs and walk back to Beckett's apartment. The lights are off in his parents' house, so I hope that means he's upstairs and not still talking with them.

At the top of the stairs, I knock twice. "It's me."

I hear movement inside, and the door opens a second later. "It's about time."

He lifts me into his arms, and I lock my elbows around his neck, relaxing into him.

"I called you an hour ago," he mumbles into my hair.

"Sorry, my phone's still in the Jeep. I had to wait for my parents to go to bed before I could sneak out."

Any other night, they wouldn't have cared, but I didn't want to risk another argument tonight.

He sets me down and shuts the door behind me, capturing my lips with a kiss. I sigh against his mouth, leaning into the door and matching his pace. After a minute, he takes my hand and tugs me across the room, and I notice the boxes beneath the window have been moved.

Some are fuller than the last time I was here. He was packing while he waited for me.

He kicks a few boxes aside, and I slide my arms

around him from behind, not ready to acknowledge his impending departure. "How did it go with your parents?"

"Once I told them everything, it went better than I thought. I think they were more upset by the idea that we might not be in love than they were that we lied to them."

"Really?" I ask, surprised.

"Yeah." He detangles my arms from him and sits on a barstool, pulling me between his legs. "I'm taking it that wasn't the case for your parents?"

"My mom just gets too invested sometimes." I shrug, eyes drifting to the boxes once more. "You're packing already?"

He presses his lips to my inner wrist. "I hadn't planned on it, but as I was unpacking my suitcase, I figured I should start now, or I never will."

I scrunch my nose, smirking as I gesture to a larger box in the corner. "Is one of those big enough for me?"

"No, I was planning to strap you to the roof of my truck." He says it as a joke, but the humor immediately dies in his eyes. His chest inflates, and he watches me regrettably. "You aren't the only thing my parents and I discussed. As it turns out, they both have to work the day I'm leaving, and it wouldn't be right to make them ask off just to drive my stuff to Boston."

His parents usually make a weekend out of his move-in—he flies to Boston with the bare necessities, gets settled in, and then they transport the rest of his boxes and stay in his guest room until everything is unpacked. Though, since it's his last year, there isn't much sense in doing that anyway. Besides, I know the drive is rough on them.

"So, you're not flying?" I ask.

He shakes his head.

"It's a ten-hour drive," I clarify, biting my lip. "That means you'll have to leave sooner."

He nods, and I'm afraid to ask my next question.

"By how much?"

He meets my gaze. "A day."

"A whole day?" I gape. "Wait, that means you're leaving Tuesday now? *Tomorrow's* our last full day together?"

He was supposed to catch his flight Wednesday evening, giving us two-and-a-half more days. Now we only have one-and-a-half.

"I'm driving through the night, so I won't leave until five." He rubs my arms. "That's why I started packing while you were gone. I figured the sooner I get it done, the more time I have to spend with you."

"Then I'll help," I offer. "We both know you suck at packing anyway."

He assesses me uncertainly. "Mac—"

"I want to," I insist, picking up a bundle of twist ties.

He sets them aside, chuckling lightly.

"Oh, I know you do. And I'd love your help." He tucks my hair behind my ears. "Something else is bothering you, though."

Embarrassment burns in my chest, and I chew on my lip. "What if you meet someone?"

He chokes on a laugh, looking as though he doesn't

have the brain capacity to process what I said. "*Meet someone*?"

"Don't laugh at me." I shove him lightly. "I know how you feel about me, but I also know that you've dated a lot of girls. What if you're there and I'm here, and you... I don't know."

He stiffens, fingers curling around mine. "You think I'd cheat on you?"

"God, *no*," I say quickly. "Not even for a second. I know who you are. I—that come out wrong."

Beckett has dated a lot of girls, yes. But not once have any of them overlapped.

"Then I don't understand. Mac, I meant it when I said you're the only one I've ever wanted."

"And I believe you," I whisper. "I guess I'm worried that I'll be holding you back."

"*You* hold me together," he counters, thumbs skating over my lips. "You've been my rock since we were kids. And you're right, I've dated a lot over the years, but *you're* the constant in my life."

He reaches to the side, picking up a twist tie and bending it in a small circle. He lifts my left hand, pressing his lips to the heel of my palm before sliding it on my ring finger.

"Now, this might not be a two-carat, oval-cut diamond with a white gold garden setting..." He licks his lips with a knowing smirk. "But it *is* my promise to you. I'm yours. I've always been yours. I'll always *be* yours."

Tears cling to my lashes, and I have to look away

from him as I swallow. "Well, shit. Now I know Poetic Beckett, too."

He wipes his thumbs beneath my eyes to catch a few stray tears. "I told you—you know every side of me there is."

I press my forehead to his, smiling despite my sadness. "And I love every one of them."

He tilts his chin up, and his warm lips envelop mine in a tender kiss that sends shivers down my spine. "So, I know I'm always the one putting it off, but we need to figure out what to tell people about us."

"What if we don't tell them anything?" I ask quietly. I've been thinking about this a lot, and no matter how we spin it, we look like frauds. "What if we let it run its course?"

"You want to keep pretending?" he asks, stunned.

"Why not?" I reason. "Our relationship is no one's business, and it's better than trying to explain the truth. We told everyone we wanted a long engagement; if we break up down the road, we can call it off then." I weave my fingers through his and hope he doesn't think I'm insane. "But if you're not okay with it—"

"No, I'm in," he says. "I never liked the idea of leaving you to deal with the fallout once I'm gone. Honestly, I would have suggested this myself, but I didn't think you'd go for it."

"Yeah, well, you're a bad influence," I taunt. "A month ago, the thought never would have crossed my mind."

He feigns offense, but before he can reply, a knock

sounds at the door. He kisses me one last time, discontented with the interruption.

"It's open," he calls, and I turn, leaning against his thigh to see who it is.

Beckett's mom steps inside, eyes darting between us in surprise. "Oh, sorry. I was coming to see if you needed help."

"Nah, Mac has me covered."

His mom nods.

"I'm sorry about lying to you," I say, hoping she doesn't hate me. My mom will get over what we did, but it's not her opinion I care about.

Mrs. Harlow raised me just as much as my own parents, and unlike them, she never let whatever argument she was having with her husband affect the way she treated me.

"It's okay, hon. You have all year to make it up to me," she says, hand on the doorknob. "Don't worry about it right now."

Then she leaves, and Beckett slides a palm over my waist to hold me to his chest. "You know she's not even mad at you, right? She chewed me out for putting you in this situation because you're an angel and *I'm* a bad influence."

"Well, if we're being fair..."

He nips at my ear, and I laugh. "Don't you *dare* say this was all my idea. Deep down, you wanted it just as much as I did."

"No comment." I close my eyes and rest my head on

his shoulder. "We're not going to get any packing done, are we?"

"We will," he says. "We just have to take breaks in between boxes."

"Oh yeah, for what?" I turn my head, and he kisses me.

"For this."

He spins me toward him, and I smile. "I think I can manage that."

"Are you sure?"

"Definitely."

Chapter Seventeen

BOXES ARE STACKED to the brim in the back of Beckett's truck, and he closes the hatch, locking the windows since he'll be stopping for gas at different exits along the highway.

We packed the remainder of his things yesterday morning, then spent the day like we always do since I didn't have to work. But it went way too fast.

The hours leading up to his departure are always the worst, and I remember him leaving his freshman year as one of the worst days of my life. I'd worried that he'd meet new friends and forget all about me, but I should have known better than to think Beckett would ever abandon me. I was stupid to think it then, and I was even more ridiculous for worrying about it the other night.

"You call us every time you stop, understand?" Mrs. Harlow says, smothering Beckett in a bear hug.

"Yeah, Mom," he agrees hugging his dad next.

Mrs. Harlow wipes under her eyes and sniffles. "You'd think the fourth time would be easier."

"Come on, let's give the kids some space," Mr. Harlow says, and they each hug their son goodbye one last time before heading inside.

Beckett doesn't say a word. He simply draws me into his arms, and I melt against him, burrowing my face in the crook of his neck.

"Why is it so much harder this time?" I ask, but we both know the answer.

Because we're so much closer, the distance feels greater.

Plus, this is his senior year. He has capstone courses and semester-long presentations that will build until graduation. He might not have a chance to call me every day or set aside time for an over-the-phone movie date when he has term deadlines.

"I'll come home as often as I can," he mumbles, swaying us slowly. "And if you're ever off for a weekend and want to fly out... I wouldn't say no."

I rise to kiss his cheek, but he turns his head, capturing my mouth instead.

"I hate leaving you," he mumbles.

A tear leaks from my eye, and I scan his features. "It's not too late to strap me to the roof."

A laugh vibrates through his chest, and he kisses me long and hard. He's right in front of me, and yet it feels like he's already gone.

"I love you," he whispers, voice thick. "The first chance I get, I'm coming home, okay?"

"Okay," I repeat as he kisses either cheek, my nose, the corners of my mouth. "I love you, too."

His lips find mine again, and his hands slide down my arms as he slowly backs away.

When we separate, longing blue eyes take me in as Beckett feels for the door of his truck, not bothering to look. "I left something on my bed for you. I'll see you soon, Mac."

I swallow the lump in my throat. "Bye, Becks."

He hoists himself into the truck and turns the ignition. I catch his eyes through the sideview mirror as he shifts into drive, and I lift a hand to wave as he starts down the hill.

I hug myself and stare after him until his taillights disappear.

Mrs. Harlow comes outside after a few minutes, and she hugs me from behind. "Would you like to stay for dinner, hon?"

I decline, wiping under my eyes. "Thanks, but I think I'm just going to grab my things and head home."

"Okay." She rubs my arms before stepping away. "Can I at least make you a plate to go? I know you two usually get dinner before he catches his flight."

"Sure, that would be great. I'll stop back over before I leave," I say, thanking her again before heading to the garage.

In Beckett's apartment, I collect my phone, purse, and keys, then stop at his bed on my way out to see what he left me.

There's a note folded on the comforter, but when I lift it, it's heavier than a regular piece of paper.

In case you miss me too much.

Taped to it is a silver key, and I slide my nail beneath the tape to remove it. I stare at the object in my hand, then close my fist around it, setting my things down and walking to the door.

I line the key up with the lock.

It's a perfect fit.

He left me a key to his apartment so I could come here to be closer to him like he does my balcony. I close the door and walk back to the bed, sliding the key around the ring that holds my car and house keys.

Climbing onto his bed, I clutch his pillow to my chest. Despite how much it smells like him, just knowing he's gone for the foreseeable future makes it feel haunted somehow.

I pick up the note to reread his words when I notice something else written on the back. I flip it over, scanning his chicken scratch.

Or if you feel like cleaning ;)

A smile splits my lips, and I fold the paper back up and stick it in my wallet for safekeeping, next to the makeshift ring he gave me. Then I rest my chin on his pillow and close my eyes, breathing in.

I don't intend to stay here long, but before I know it,

it's pitch-black outside and I haven't moved a muscle. There isn't a single light on in his apartment, and it takes me a while to find the remote so I can turn on the TV. Even though I'd rather watch a cheesy rom-com, I opt for something he'd enjoy and pretend I'm not alone watching it.

Then, around three-thirty in the morning, my phone lights up with a text, and I grapple for it, opening his message.

Beckett: *Just got here. I miss you.*
Me: *I miss you, too. Thanks for the key.*
Beckett: *I meant what I said about cleaning my place.*
Me: *What else do you think I'm still doing here at three a.m.?*
Beckett: *Are you really?*

I snap a picture of the TV.

Me: *I missed you too much.*
Beckett: *How much time is left?*
Me: *Not enough. Besides, you just drove ten hours; you need sleep.*
Beckett: *You're right. Tomorrow night?*
Me: *Only if I can choose the movie.*
Beckett: *Deal. Goodnight, Mac.*

I text back and set my phone aside, wishing more than anything that he'd say to hell with sleep and call me anyway, but he can't. This is a big year for him, and I won't be the one to distract him from his priorities.

My phone lights up with another message, but this one isn't from Beckett.

Mrs. Harlow: *Leftovers are at the bottom of the stairs. I know he gave you a key—you're welcome whenever you want. Goodnight, sweetheart.*

At first, I'm surprised she's still awake at this hour, but then I remember Beckett just got home, and there's no way in hell she'd go to bed without knowing he made it to Boston in one piece.

I throw the covers off and jog down the stairs. The garage is air-conditioned and much cooler than his apartment, so I quickly grab the food and lock the garage door, shivering as I run back upstairs. I peel the foil off a paper plate and consume the piece of chicken and pile of mashed potatoes—leftovers from the meal she sent Beckett back to school with so he wouldn't have to worry about food until this weekend.

When I'm finished, I toss the plate in the trash and wash the fork, making a note to return it to her tomorrow. Then I hunker down on Beckett's bed and close my eyes.

I miss him like hell, and it's only been a few hours. But I know we'll make this work. We have to. And after texting with him, receiving a key to his apartment... I feel better.

We may be over six hundred miles apart, but he's with me wherever we are.

So, no matter the distance between us or the worst missing him will bring, I know with more certainty than I've ever had toward anything, we'll only come out stronger.

"Order up!"

My feet carry me behind the bar, where I grab a steaming hot plate with a cheeseburger and home fries, then hustle toward table five.

"Here's your burger—the cornbread should be done any minute," I say, motioning for the pitcher of water Hannah passes with. She hands it over without a second glance, heading to greet a table that was just seated. I refill my customer's glass and set a small stack of napkins in the center of the table. "Can I get you anything else?"

"A few packets of sugar for my coffee?" he asks, nodding toward the empty basket that's usually filled with an assortment of brands.

"Yes, of course. Sorry about that." I take the basket, deposit the pitcher behind the bar, and head straight toward the kitchen to replenish the sugar.

"Mac, can you take that pasta to table seventeen?" Hannah asks, tossing an empty ketchup bottle in the trash and peeling the seal off a new one.

I finish filling the sugar and swerve past her to grab the bowl. "Gotcha."

I deliver it to the customer, retrieve a fresh slice of cornbread, then head back to my table, placing the basket of sugar where it belongs.

"Oh, thanks. I just took some from the booth behind me," the man says, and I glance at the empty booth in question, which now only has two packets of sugar left because he took five.

I force a smile, grabbing that basket now that it needs a refill as well. "No problem, enjoy your meal."

After filling it, I slip behind the bar to wait at the counter where the cooks deposit meals as they're finished.

"What's taking so long?" I ask Hannah, who's leaning against the wall.

Three burgers are waiting, but there aren't fries on any of the plates.

"Cooper dropped a batch on the floor."

I close my eyes. "You're kidding. The whole batch? He just made them—"

"Fifteen minutes ago, I know." She stifles a yawn.

It's rush hour and we've been the only servers all day because whoever else was scheduled didn't show. And, because so many college kids are going back to school, it seems every family in town has come here for a farewell meal.

We haven't had more than three empty tables at a time all day, and I'm pretty sure I've worn holes in the soles of my shoes running back and forth.

"Hopefully things will slow down in the next hour," Hannah says, yawning again. "Sorry, I closed last night because Tay didn't show, so I'm only physically here right now."

"Do you think she was scheduled today, too?" I ask, fuming. I hate people who let personal feuds get in the way of doing their job. I haven't spoken to Tay since the barbeque, and I don't expect her to reach out anytime soon. She's domineering and meddlesome, but she can't take it when someone pushes back.

She shrugs. "I haven't looked, but it seems likely. I had a shift with her and Elle while you were gone, and she didn't speak two words to me the whole time. I told her one of her tables didn't get their milkshake and she ignored me. Elle thinks she's mad we became friends."

"What? Like I stole you from her?"

Hannah shakes her head tiredly. "No idea. She and I were never close to begin with, but she's definitely a little obsessive."

"Well, she's also cruel if she purposefully hung us out to dry today," I grumble, resting my head against the wall.

Beau, one of the cooks, steps in front of the window and folds his arms on the counter. "You talking about Tay?"

Hannah and I exchange a glance, and she licks her lips, speaking casually. "Yeah, we were wondering who was scheduled today."

"Well, her cubby was cleaned out, so I'm assuming she's not coming back."

Cooper calls for Beau from the fryer, and he heads to help him transport the fries to the plates as quickly as possible. Once they're plated, Hannah and I deliver them to the correct tables, and I pray the burgers aren't cold. I did not suffer all day to receive shitty tips for something that wasn't my fault.

The remainder of the evening goes much like the first half of the day did, and when the tables are wiped, floors are cleaned, and all appliances are turned off, I sit on a chair to give my feet a rest.

I walked here because I knew it would still be light out when my shift ended, but my feet are scolding me for that decision right now.

"Pete's in his office," Hannah says, closing the door to her cubby. "Says he wants to see you."

I crack my neck and roll my ankles with a sigh. "Okay, thanks. Is there any chance you could drop me off at my house? My stupid ass thought it would be a good idea to walk today."

She laughs. "Yeah, no problem. I'll get the car started so we don't suffocate."

Mustering some energy, I walk down the hall and hang my apron, then knock on the boss's office door.

"Come in," he says, and I hear him stand from his desk. I close the door behind me, so tired I can hardly stand straight.

"You wanted to see me?" I ask, hoping he makes this quick so I can go home.

Pete threads his fingers in front of him. "Tayler Tate stopped in this morning and asked not to be scheduled with you anymore."

"What?" My jaw slacks, and I quickly cover my shock, clearing my throat. "Did she say why?"

He waves his hand dismissively. "She said she can't work with someone she doesn't trust."

My chest burns, and I suppress my frustration, twiddling my thumbs. "What did you tell her?"

"The same thing I'm telling you: There is no drama in my kitchen. You either put your differences aside during your shifts or you're gone, and she obviously wasn't capable of that, or she wouldn't have come to me."

"You fired her." I swallow, remembering what Beau said about her cubby being cleaned out. "You're firing me."

He nods. "I'm sorry, Mac. But like I said, I don't put up with workplace drama, and I certainly don't let it affect the other servers like it did when she didn't show up last night."

"Pete, I've never been *anything* but professional."

"I know, and it pains me to let you go, but I refuse to risk residual problems by keeping you on. We live in a close-knit community—one word to the wrong person could mean a huge loss in business if someone decides to boycott your services for Tay."

"That's ridiculous," I argue. "I'm sorry, but it is. I stay until close more often than anyone else and never complain, I have the highest customer satisfaction rate, and I've worked here consistently *without issue* since I was sixteen. Not to mention, I've only asked off twice in almost five years."

He can't rely on his other servers like he does me.

Just last week, one of the seasonal hires called in sick so she could get drunk. The only reason I know that is because she was caught underage drinking and lost her license. That means she has no transportation and can only get here twice a week.

But he didn't fire *her* because that's apparently not what he considers drama.

If I'd known I could get a free pass for irresponsibility, I could have had a lot more fun over the years.

"You're right. You are my best server. But as I've said—"

"No drama," I interrupt.

"Look, I'll have your week's paycheck by Sunday. If you'd like to finish out your shifts, I'll compensate you for the additional time," he offers, though I can see right through him.

He's already short two servers, and if I don't finish out the week, he's put in a tough spot. Ironically, the only person truly causing drama here is him.

"If you were worried about being understaffed, you should have thought of that before you fired me for no reason," I say, heading out the door. I pause in the hallway, unable to help myself. "And you should know that both of my parents and the Harlows are regulars here. Though, I doubt they will be after today."

I grab my things from my cubby—extra ponytail holders and bobby pins, my purse, and the box of granola bars I keep for when we're busy and I don't have time for a full meal during my break.

I don't bother to stop and look around before I leave. If I do, my last memories of this place will be of me leaving it, and I'd rather savor the memory of a hectic day working alongside Hannah than the betrayal I feel right now.

Hannah's parked along the sidewalk waiting for me, and I take a few breaths, willing myself not to cry. Her window's open, so I stop briefly, avoiding eye contact.

"Hey, I think I'm just going to walk after all. Sorry for making you wait."

She looks up, and I train my eyes ahead, starting toward the road.

I hear her door open, and I close my eyes as she jogs around the vehicle. "Five minutes ago, you looked like you'd rather stick pins in your eyes than walk home. What happened? Why did Pete want to see you?"

My lip quivers, and I dig my teeth into it, hoping she doesn't notice the tears welling in my eyes. "Tay got me fired."

Her brown eyes widen, and she blinks several times before my words fully sink in. "How?"

I tell her what happened, and the more I talk, the harder it is to hold back my tears.

When I'm finished, her tongue skates across the edges of her teeth, and before I can process what she's doing, she marches back toward the diner.

"Where are you going?"

She waves her hand dismissively as she swings open the front door. "I'll be right back. Wait in the car."

"Hannah, I already gave him a piece of my mind, please don't make it worse."

Too late. She's already inside.

I cross my arms and lean against the passenger door, waiting anxiously. She emerges two minutes later, motioning for me to get in the car. I do, and when she gets behind the wheel and puts it in drive without a word, I finally speak up. "What did you say?"

She glances at me simply, then looks both ways before turning onto my street. "I quit."

"You—*what*? You said you needed that job. You said no one else was hiring."

"No one was," she says. "I was offered a job somewhere else while you were gone. It pays the same and I'd still be serving, but it's closer to home. The only reason I considered turning it down was because I was making friends here and liked working with you. But if Pete would treat *you* like that, after all you've done for him over the years, no one is safe. I won't work for someone who would do that. Tay created a problem and he dealt with her appropriately. But you did nothing wrong."

Maybe not, but I just said goodbye to my best friend and my job of five years in under twenty-four hours. I feel like my world is slowly crumbling around me, and the only person I want to talk about it with is starting his senior year. The last thing I want is to bog him down with my problems.

So instead, I let Hannah drive me home in silence, and I try my hardest not to cry.

Chapter Eighteen

WHEN HANNAH DROPS me off at my house, I sit on the front steps for half an hour before I will myself to go inside. I haven't seen my parents since Mom found out the engagement was fake, and I assume Mrs. Harlow told them about the key since neither of them texted me in a panic when I didn't come home.

Dad is on the couch watching Thursday Night Football with a beer in one hand and a big bowl of popcorn on his lap. When he hears me come in, he mutes the game, craning his neck to see me.

"And here I thought with Beckett gone, I'd get to see my daughter again," he says, holding the bowl out to me.

I slide my purse off my shoulder and drop down in the chair beside the couch. I dip my fingers into the bowl and collect a handful of buttery popcorn. Then I gesture to the extra beer waiting for him.

He suppresses a smirk, pushing it toward me with his foot. "Take it."

Twisting the cap off, I take a long swig before ripping the bandage off. "I just got fired."

His eyes tear from the TV, wide with shock. "What the hell happened?"

"Literally nothing," I say, taking another gulp. "Tay has been... a handful, to say the least. But apparently, she told Pete she didn't want to be scheduled with me anymore."

"And Pete refuses to tolerate workplace drama," he says, knowing the policy all too well after the number of servers who have come and gone over the years. "Still, her actions don't speak for you."

"Yeah, I know." I bite my lip. "Do you know anyone hiring? Preferably who isn't close with Pete?"

"I might." He sits forward, placing his beer on a coaster. "I've never had a problem with your job at the diner because you work so hard, but maybe you should take this opportunity to find a more sustainable one where you're not working paycheck to paycheck."

I plop a few pieces of popcorn into my mouth, chewing while I work up a response.

The diner wasn't a career job, and I was never going to work there forever, but it was comfortable. I think a part of me hoped that when Pete retired in a few years, I could convince him to sell the diner to me. I would have been the prime candidate.

"You're right," I whisper, staring at his feet propped on the coffee table. "But I at least want something short term while I search."

Otherwise, I'll turn into the sad girl who drinks alone on her balcony and waits for her boyfriend to call.

Days like today at the diner are the worst, but they keep me busy enough that I don't have time to let my thoughts wander toward how much I miss Beckett. It's why I always volunteer to handle the back-to-school rush week.

Dad picks up his beer and tips the neck toward me. "*That,* I can help you with. I'll ask around in the morning and see if anyone needs a hand."

"Thanks, Dad." I rise from the couch, throwing the rest of the popcorn in my mouth. I hesitate to leave though, thinking back to the other night. "And thanks for taking the heat off of me with Mom. You didn't have to do that."

She had no idea he knew the engagement was fake, and she never needed to.

"If I hadn't, she would have said something she couldn't take back." He waves his hand, eyes drawn back to the TV. "I told you, I don't understand why you had to lie, but I knew that kid was in love with you long before you did. Besides, it seems like it all worked out, didn't it?"

I lift a shoulder, nodding somberly. "Yeah, I suppose it did. Have you talked to Mom yet today?"

"Once or twice. Not about you, though."

I purse my lips, deciding not to push it.

If they talked *once or twice,* that means they argued for hours about my lie and how he kept it from her. When I was younger, he used to refrain from fighting with her in front of me, but as I got older, it became harder to hide.

I was nine when I realized that every time they stuck me outside to play or sent me to Beckett's house, it was code for "get out, we want to scream at each other but don't want you to overhear."

Eventually, I realized the ghosts and demons I was so scared of as a child weren't monsters under my bed at all, but my parents arguing in their bedroom on the other side of the house.

Somehow, I think knowing the truth would have been less traumatic. In elementary school, I was invited to a slumber party, and when the girls put on *Casper the Friendly Ghost,* I cried so hard her parents sent me home because I was "ruining the other girls' fun."

My parents never let me watch those movies because the supernatural freaked me out so much. Little did they know, it was because I thought I was being haunted every night. But no. It was just my parents' marriage scarring me for life.

Upstairs, I slide open the door to my balcony, easing onto a chair.

Beckett hasn't texted me since this morning, but I know he had to purchase his textbooks and meet with his advisor today. She moved up their meeting since he came earlier than intended. Plus, he knew I was working all day.

Holding up my beer, I snap a picture, making sure I get the railing and his empty chair in the frame. Then I click to edit the photo, drawing a wonky stick figure in the chair beside me.

Twenty minutes pass before he replies with two simple words: *Ten minutes.*

I have no idea what that means, but I watch the clock intensely.

My phone lights up with a call, and I smile, trying to sound happy even though I want to cry again. "How was your first day back?"

"Good, it was—" he hesitates, then groans. "Who am I kidding? Mac, it was awful. I want to die. The group advisor for my capstone course gave us homework, and classes haven't even started yet. And if I think about you any more during the day, I'm going to manifest a doppelgänger."

I snort a laugh. "You're the one who didn't want to be a college dropout."

"Yeah, well, I'm rethinking my stance," he jokes, and the smile in his voice is contagious. "How was work?"

I tip my head toward the sky, gritting my teeth. "Oh, you know, the usual."

"That bad?" he teases.

I scoff but refrain from telling him the truth. He has enough on his plate. "Worse, but now I'm home and talking to you. So, it's not all that bad."

"Speaking of me being the highlight of your day," he begins, and I laugh out loud, wishing I could hug him. "I was thinking, you should fly out next weekend if you can. Even if I'm doing homework, it would be worth it to spend a few days with you."

I squeeze my eyes shut, heart heavy. "Becks, I can't."

"Why not? I hate this."

"Me, too, and that's exactly why I can't. If I fly out this soon, then it will be like we're saying goodbye all over again. Besides, you already said how busy you are. Next weekend might be even worse."

And I might have a new job by then. I can't start off my first week by asking for a long weekend.

But still... the thought of turning down an opportunity to see him...

"What about Labor Day weekend? You have that Monday off, don't you?" I ask, figuring that's two weeks to get used to being apart and fall into some sort of routine. It's always hard when he leaves, but this is an entirely different kind of hurt. Missing him as my boyfriend is so much worse than missing my best friend.

"Are you saying you'll come?" he asks, guarded hope lingering in his tone.

"I'm saying I'll ask my parents if they'll cover my flight because we both know neither of us can afford it. But my mom is still mad, so no promises."

"Well, if they don't, I'm sure we could scrounge up enough money between the two of us," he insists, and his enthusiasm makes my heart soar.

"Yeah, one way. I'd have to hitchhike back."

"Not if I don't let you leave," he teases. "Wait, what about the diner? Don't you usually take a few shifts that weekend since no one else wants to?"

I swallow the lump in my throat, hating that I chose to lie to him. "I'll... figure it out."

Beckett is quiet for a minute. "Is something wrong?"

I shake my head, exhaling shakily. "No, everything's fine. I just miss you. It's harder this time."

"Yeah, I know what you mean," he says, voice lowering an octave. "But once I graduate, it'll be you and me. Nothing between us."

"Except all of your job opportunities in God knows what states."

"Since when is the girl who watches more romance movies than anyone I've ever met a pessimist?"

"How dare you, I am not a pessimist," I gape, pretending to be offended. "I'm realistic. There's a difference."

He sighs, and I picture his blue eyes rolling back in his head. "Well, stop it. It's depressing."

"Ignoring the truth doesn't make it go away," I reason, puckering my lips. Beckett may want to avoid thinking about the inevitable, but it's all I'm going to focus on until the day comes when a job either drives a wedge between us or doesn't.

Shit, I really am a pessimist.

"It's only nine-thirty, do you still want to watch a movie tonight?" I ask, changing the subject to one that's less disheartening.

Beckett agrees, and I down the last few sips of beer and head inside, tossing the bottle in my trashcan.

"Okay, go to Prime Video."

"You already know what you want to watch?" he asks warily. "That's never good for me."

I snicker. "It's called *Letters to Juliette*. You'll love it."

"I... can pretend to."

"You can *pretend* you're pretending to," I counter. "But I'll know the truth."

"And what's the truth?"

I lie back on my bed, typing the movie title in the search bar. "You're a softy."

"Only for you."

I lick my lips with a smile. "I can live with that. Do you have it ready?"

"Yep. On three?" he asks, and I count backward, both of us hitting play when we reach one.

Chapter Nineteen

MY KNUCKLES RAP ON MY PARENTS' bedroom door, and they both look up, surprised by my presence. I can't remember the last time I came downstairs before bed, even to say goodnight to them.

I spent half of the day trying to figure out what I want to do with the rest of my life, and the other half debating how to ask my parents for money. I struck out in both ventures. When I brought up going to Boston during dinner, my mom all but blew a gasket. Needless to say, if I book a flight, it won't be on her dime.

"Can we talk?" I ask, leaning against the doorframe. My dad mutes the TV, though his eyes remain glued to the screen.

"That depends," Mom says, shifting her glasses down her nose and setting her Kindle aside. "Are you here to apologize or ask for more money?"

I cringe. My dad and I may be square, but I haven't

had a conversation with my mom about the fake engagement yet. Mrs. Harlow told me that they split the guest list and called everyone to cancel the engagement dinner, blaming it on Beckett's early departure. Realistically, we still could have made it work, but regardless, we put our parents in a position to lie, and there's nothing I regret more about this arrangement.

"To apologize," I concede crossing the room to sit on the edge of their king-size bed. "Beckett and I lied, and we shouldn't have, but ultimately, I think we both wanted a chance to get closer in a way that wouldn't jeopardize our friendship."

Mom raises an eyebrow. "And here I thought my *pushiness* was to blame."

"Partly," I say sheepishly. "I made my own choices, and I'll own that, but I never would have considered lying if you hadn't threatened Tony on me. You always said how unnatural it was for me to be single for so long, then you were so excited about me and Beckett..." I drop my gaze. "I'd already fabricated a boyfriend at the airport, I figured it wouldn't be a stretch for you to believe I'd been talking about him."

She sucks on her teeth, eyeing my dad. "Give us a minute, will you?"

He grunts, picks up his phone, and heads to the living room. Though, as annoyed as he acts, I'd bet money he's thrilled to have escaped this conversation.

When we hear the TV turn on, Mom sits forward, eyeing me apprehensively.

"I'm sorry if I made you feel like you had to lie to

me," she says, surprising me with her honesty. My mother is a lot of things, but 'easy to apologize to' isn't usually one of them. "I only pushed you so hard because deep down I knew you were waiting on Beckett. He has always loved you—anyone with eyes could see it—but I didn't know if he'd ever be ready *to* love you." She takes my hand. "Mac, I guess what I'm trying to say is... I was afraid you would waste your life waiting on a man who would never come around, then end up settling for someone you don't love when the truth sank in."

"You mean, settle like you did," I realize, lowering my voice. The TV volume is loud, and my dad isn't one to eavesdrop, but still, I would never want to hurt him.

My mom shuts her eyes. "I was so independent when I was young. I shut down every man I ever met, waiting for the one who would sweep me off my feet. I love your father, even if it doesn't seem like it at times, and he *did* sweep me off my feet when we met."

"But?" I ask hoarsely.

"But he shouldn't have proposed, and I shouldn't have said yes. Our flame had already fizzled, and we *both* settled for what was there at the moment." She touches my face. "If not Beckett, I wanted you to meet someone while you were young, so you'd never be put in that position. But don't you dare think I have any regrets because if I hadn't married your father, we wouldn't have you, Ryan..."

"Two grandkids you hardly know," I add, saying what she needs to hear, even if she doesn't like it.

She purses her lips, folding her hands in her lap. "I

should have been more supportive when you went to see him. I never asked how it went."

"I didn't expect you to." I shrug. She wasn't necessarily unsupportive, but her lack of enthusiasm told me all I needed to know.

"What are they like?" she asks tentatively.

I start to describe them to her, then change my mind, slipping my phone out of my back pocket and holding it between us. "I promised I'd call once a week to talk to the kids. Why don't you see for yourself?"

"Where's Becky?" Emmy asks, bouncing in and out of the frame. There's a mozzarella stick clamped in her pudgy hand, and she rips a hunk off, squinting as though Beckett might appear behind me at any moment.

"He's away at school right now, but next time I see him, I'll make sure we call so you can say 'hi.'"

Satisfied with that, she munches on her snack. Ryan chuckles in the background, taking the phone from her. "Okay, it's almost time for bed. Say 'goodnight' to Aunt Mac."

"G'night, Aunt Mac," Emmy says as Eli peeks his head around to see the screen, which his sister has hogged the entire call.

"'Night, Aunt Mac. We miss you," he says, waving with a sweet smile.

"I miss you guys, too. Goodnight."

Angela appears and says hello before she wrangles

the kids for bedtime, briefly reprimanding Ryan for allowing Emory to have a snack so late.

He and my mom talked for half an hour before he put the kids on for me, and although they haven't told me what was said, I didn't hear any yelling. Mom's eyes were also misty when she handed me the phone, which means there's a chance they'll have a relationship again someday.

"I'm sorry for the ambush," I say, closing my bedroom door. "It was a spur-of-the-moment decision. I hope I didn't put you in an awkward spot."

"You didn't," he says, propping the phone on his kitchen counter. "I don't know what you did to her, but I think that was the most meaningful conversation we've had in over a decade."

My chest constricts.

"We were talking about my engagement when it came up," I begin, hands sweating. "Speaking of, there's something I need to tell you. Something I should have told you from the start."

"You're not engaged, are you?" he asks, and I'm taken aback.

"You knew?"

"No, but I suspected."

"How?" I ask, not sure if I'm more surprised by his admittance or the fact that he doesn't appear to hate me for lying.

"For starters, no one proposes at the mall. At least, not without some serious significance behind the gesture," he says, and I can't help but laugh because he has a point. "You never wore or mentioned a ring, you were stingy with details regarding your relationship, and when I first called you about visiting us, you said you 'weren't in the mood' to talk about the engagement. Angela has had five friends get engaged—some more than once—none of whom ever turned down an opportunity to brag. Meanwhile, neither of you mentioned what you wanted your future to look like. Eventually, I put the pieces together."

"Why didn't you say anything?" I ask, stupefied by his keen observation. If I ever need a lawyer, I know who to call.

"It was obvious the two of you were in love, and I knew he was like family to you. I decided to let you come clean on your own time."

He says all of this so calmly that I have a hard time processing his words. I can't believe he's not furious.

"Are you sure you weren't adopted?" I ask finally. "Because no one in this family deals with things that reasonably."

Ryan rolls his eyes. "There's a good chance both of us were kidnapped at birth."

I throw my head back with a laugh, and then we spend the next hour talking about life. He tells me stories about the kids growing up, how he fell in love with Angela during college, and even asks how Beckett is doing.

We talk about everything and nothing at all, and I can't believe I missed out on getting to know him growing up.

If he had let himself, I think he would have been an amazing brother to me back then.

More than that, I'm glad he's trying to be one now, and because of his efforts, I have the opportunity to be an aunt to his remarkable children.

Chapter Twenty

THE LAST SEVERAL days have been the longest of my life. Between searching for jobs and waiting for fleeting phone calls with Beckett, I feel more overwhelmed than during the busiest days at the diner.

Rain pours down in buckets outside, and I keep checking my phone, having given up job searches for the night. Beckett usually calls around nine, but it's ten thirty, and he hasn't so much as texted me.

I curl up on my bed and close my eyes, trying not to be too sad about it. His workload is insane, and he has no idea I haven't been working twenty-four-seven.

I must doze off at some point because I startle when my phone vibrates. I rub my eyes, squinting at the bright screen to see Beckett's name flashing across it.

"Is everything okay?" I ask, groggily. I'm slightly worried that he's calling so late.

"Why didn't you tell me you were fired?" he asks, and I drop back on my pillow, relief flooding me.

"Becks, you just gave me a heart attack. I thought something was wrong."

"Why didn't you tell me?" he reiterates, static breaking up the call.

I sigh, turning on my lamp and propping myself up in bed. "Because it's just a job—"

He cuts me off, but I struggle to understand what he says because of the storm raging outside. "Not to you. That place was your third home after me and your parents. I know I have a lot going on, but you can still tell me what's happening in your life. I shouldn't have to find out from Gabe."

"I know, but I didn't want to burden you."

He says something, but thunder rumbles overhead and cuts him off.

"Becks, I can't hear you."

"Co—"

I check the volume of my phone to make sure it's turned up all the way, but all I can hear is static.

"Are you there?"

Thunder booms again, and lightning strikes across the sky. He doesn't say anything for a while, and just when I think I've lost him, his voice cuts through the silence. "MacKenzie, come outside."

I sit up straight and set my phone aside as my eyes skate toward the balcony.

There's no way...

Jumping to my feet, I run to the door, slide it open, and step out into the rain. My eyes scan the dark yard, and I see a figure by the tree beneath my balcony.

"Are you insane?" I yell, moving to the railing as he starts climbing. He uses the windowsill to guide his body toward the balcony, and I reach out, grabbing his arm as his foot slips. I keep a tight grip on him as he swings a leg over the railing, and before I can take him in, he moves to wrap me in his arms. I hug him close, shuddering as the rain soaks through my hair and clothes. "What the hell are you doing here?"

"I couldn't get a flight," is all he says, and I shove him backward, then grip the front of his shirt.

"You *drove* here?" I gape, searching his expression, but I don't find an ounce of regret. "It's after midnight, don't you have class tomorrow?"

"Not until eleven. If I drive all night, I'll make it in time." He strokes my cheeks, a soft smile on his lips.

"Becks, that's twenty hours in a car in less than a day."

"And seeing you is worth every second of the drive," he assures me, eyes drifting from my eyes to my lips. "I realized something I never told you while I was in class today."

I choke on a laugh. "You couldn't tell me over the phone?"

"I know how much you romance junkies like your grand gestures." His hands side down the length of my arms, pressing them to his chest. "No one has ever told me I'm scared of commitment."

I tilt my head, not following. "I don't understand. The *entire* reason for our engagement was so you could prove that you're capable of commitment."

"I lied," he says, keeping my arms pressed to his chest with one hand while the other skims over my lips.

"Why?" I ask, slightly overwhelmed. "All of your relationships ended because of—"

"*You*, Mac. Every girl I've ever dated told me that I was *too* committed. To you. They all said they felt like they came second to our friendship. I was so hopelessly in love with you that I subconsciously sabotaged every relationship I've ever been in." He searches my gaze desperately. "When someone misinterpreted the proposal at the mall, I thought that pretending to be a couple might get you to look at me the way I've always looked at you."

There aren't words in the English language to describe the roller coaster of emotions rumbling inside of me.

"Mac, you're so worried that we're going to fall apart that you can't see how strong we are together. I want to be with you. I want to build a life with you. And I know you're afraid of where mine will take me when I graduate, but if we're really serious about us, then we'll make those decisions together."

"You can't base your life off of me." I blink rapidly, rain coasting off my eyelashes.

"Nothing in my life will matter if you're not in it, and I know you feel the same."

"Of course I do." I grip his face in my hands, gaze trailing over every divot. "You know, you ruined every relationship I've ever been in, too, don't you?"

He tucks my hair behind my ears. "Why? Because I threatened them all?"

I purse my lips with a head shake, stretching so we're closer in height. "Because deep down, I knew you were the only man I was ever going to love."

My lips flirt with his, and the slightest tilt of his chin brings them together as his arms circle my back and press me against him. I kiss him desperately, making up for every second we lost since he left. Every second we wasted being scared of this thing between us that has turned out to be the best part of my life. His kiss gives me life, and his mouth moves against mine like it's all he's wanted since the second he left.

"When do you have to head back?" I ask between kisses, pulling him out of the rain. I shiver when the air conditioning hits me, and he collects me in his arms, lips trailing down the side of my neck.

"Half an hour," he says, and I can't help but wish it was longer than that. His mouth captures mine in another long, sensual kiss that makes my blood simmer, and then he rests his forehead against mine, fingers combing through my hair.

Water drips off us in steady streams, so I jog to the bathroom to grab some towels for us to stand on, then hand him one to squeeze the moisture out of his clothes.

"Are you going to be okay driving that long in one day?" I ask, a little worried about him leaving so late and in such bad weather. Not to mention, exhaustion is etched all over his face.

He dips his chin and captures my lips in reassurance. "I'll be fine."

I nod, figuring I'll argue that when it comes time for him to leave. "Do you have a change of clothes?"

He flattens his lips. "They never show this part in the movies, do they?"

I snicker, wiping rainwater off his face. "No, I guess they don't. I still have your jacket in my Jeep. That's better than nothing."

"There might be a pair of shorts in my gym bag, but I can't remember."

I hold out my hand and motion for him to toss me his keys. "I'll check."

Running downstairs, I grab an umbrella before getting his fleece jacket from my car. Then I scour his gym bag for a pair of shorts, which I thankfully find crumpled in a ball at the bottom. I head back inside, tossing the dry clothes on the bed and rummaging through my drawer to find a pair of sweats.

"I can throw your wet clothes in the dryer for a quick cycle," I offer, to which he agrees.

He changes in my bathroom, and I slip into my closet to strip out of my clothes, which are stuck to me like a second layer of skin. Goose bumps rise on my arms, and I dry myself with a towel before stepping into a pair of pants and putting on a t-shirt that's hanging to my left.

When I exit the closet, Beckett has already picked up the wet towels, so I show him to the laundry room, where I throw his clothes in the dryer with a few others to help sop up the moisture. I save the towels for later, figuring they'll only hinder the process, and we head back upstairs to my bedroom.

Grabbing a few extra blankets, Beckett and I snuggle under the covers, and I soak in the body heat emitting from him as he envelops me in his arms.

We don't say much of anything. Instead, Beckett sets an alarm so we don't lose track of time, and we hold on to each other until our brief intermission from reality comes to an end.

I bury my face in his chest, trying not to worry about when it does. Every once in a while, he pulls back to kiss me, whether it be my cheek, forehead, nose, or lips, and I absorb each touch like oxygen I need to breathe.

The alarm pierces the air, and I whimper, holding him tighter. "Don't go."

"Don't tempt me," he murmurs, nudging my chin so he can kiss me. "You know I'd never leave your side if I didn't have to."

I nod. "But you have to."

"Yeah, but at least I get to see you again Labor Day weekend," he says, a small smile playing on his lips.

I lift my head off the pillow, eyeing him suspiciously. "You scrounged up six hundred dollars for a roundtrip flight?"

"Better," he muses. "Ryan's flying us out to Oklahoma."

My jaw drops and I sit up straight, wrapping my fingers around his. "You're messing with me."

"Nope. He said you mentioned our plans, so he got my number from your dad and called to see if I could make it work. I asked him not to tell you so I could see *that exact* look on your face."

I let out a squeal, leaping onto him and rocking back and forth.

His laughter rings in my ears and he kisses my cheek, warm lips sending shivers down my spine when he speaks. "I told you we'd make this work."

"I never doubted you."

Every day we make it work. By talking, by texting, by making plans to see each other even when we don't have a second to spare.

That's effort.

Yet, it's not really an effort at all when being with him is the most important part of my life.

Epilogue

THE MALL DOORS SLIDE OPEN, and Beckett drags me into the empty space, graduation gown flowing as he rushes down the hall. Most stores have closed for the night, security gates pulled down in front of them to prohibit entry, but there are still a few open.

"Becks, they close in fifteen minutes, and we have a reservation at nine," I say, trying not to trip in my heels. "Let's come back tomorrow."

Beckett groans, turns, then grabs my face between his hands. "We'll be out of here in five, I promise."

"If we're late, your parents are going to kill us," I warn, continuing to follow him anyway.

He graduated college this evening, and I flew to Boston with his parents to watch him receive his diploma. We're staying the weekend to help him pack up his life and are supposed to meet for dinner to celebrate, so I had to ask off work for the weekend.

There was an opening at the café where Carlyle

works, and he got me a managerial position with the promise that, when the boss retires at the end of the year, I'm next in line to take over.

"Trust me, they'll be fine. My dad's birthday is on Sunday, and I forgot to get him a gift. I don't know if we'll be able to slip away again before then." He glances behind him, noticing a restroom sign on one of the walls. "I have to run to the bathroom, but look over the list and see if any of the stores are still open. I'll catch up with you in a minute."

"But—"

He cuts me off with a kiss, then backs toward a hallway to my left. "You're the best."

I stare after him in disbelief, then grumble under my breath, unfolding the list he forced into my hand.

Make dinner reservation
Pick up roses
Stop at the mall
Ask Mac to marry me

My heart stalls, and I touch my fingers to my lips as I reread the last item three more times. Ironically, the first thought I have is that he accidentally gave me the wrong list, but then I sense movement behind me. My fingers tremble as I turn to find Beckett on one knee.

"What do you say, Mac?" he asks, fumbling to open the velvet ring box. But I hardly notice the diamond. It's his eyes I can't tear my gaze away from. "Want to spend the rest of your life being my best friend?"

I struggle to find my voice as I reach to touch his cheek.

"Yeah, I'd like that," I whisper, tugging him to his feet and flinging myself into his arms. He catches me easily and spins around, lips capturing mine as he sets me down, ring box digging into my hip.

"I love you," he murmurs, forehead pressed against mine as he feels for my left hand, maneuvering the ring from the box and sliding it onto my finger.

"I love you, too," I wheeze, finally noticing the diamond. "Holy shit, that's a lot nicer than the twisty."

Beckett chokes on a laugh, and my hands frame his face, brushing over the dimples that groove his cheeks.

"My parents loaned me the money," he explains. "I couldn't wait any longer, but I didn't want just any ring."

I glance at the diamond glittering off my finger—the exact one I told my mom he bought me last July. "It's perfect."

"I got a job offer at a firm thirty minutes from Richlynd. Junior financial advisor." He pockets the ring box and slides his hands over my hips. "It's going to be demanding at first, but we'll be together."

"What? Becks, that's fantastic," I breathe, chest expanding with joy. "Are you sure it's what you want?"

He nods, gaze flitting across my face. "It's everything I want."

Warm lips close around mine, but I groan, pulling back despite how much I want to kiss him and say to hell with our obligations. A little dizzy from his kiss, I swallow, trying to form a coherent sentence. "Your parents. Dinner."

"I lied," he smirks. "The reservation isn't until nine-thirty." He kisses me again. "And I told our parents we'd be a little late."

I raise an eyebrow, thinking he misspoke. "Our?"

He didn't. "Yours insisted on being here since the last time I proposed was a little anticlimactic. They flew in during the ceremony."

I puff out my bottom lip and arch my back to see him better. "It's a good thing I didn't say no, then."

He laughs, then takes my hand, thumb coasting over my ring finger before he tugs me toward the exit. We head outside into the warm night. It's only early May, but the weather warns of a humid summer to come.

Beckett walks me to the passenger side of his truck, where the bouquet of roses he gave me after the ceremony sits on my seat, but instead of opening the door for me, he moves forward until I'm pressed against it.

He wears a knowing smile, face lit by the lamp post a few feet away, and I run my fingers through his hair. "What now?"

"Did I mention I don't start my new job until the fall?" he asks, already knowing he didn't.

I bite my lip. "Are you saying we have one last summer to ourselves?"

"Mmhmm..." He lowers his face. "Your mom even mentioned adding me to the family vacation roster."

"Did she now?"

"She did," he confirms, mouth finding mine again in the empty mall parking lot. He kisses me until our lips are swollen and I can hardly catch my breath. Then, in a raspy voice, he asks, "Can you believe it took us this long to get here?"

My fingers sweep across his collarbone and to the back of his neck. "I'm just glad that we did," I admit, not caring about the specifics.

Beckett watches me like I'm his whole world, and it strikes me to my core. I wouldn't care if it had taken another decade for us to realize how we felt about each other.

There is nothing more real, more *fulfilling*, than being so unapologetically in love with your best friend that they occupy every vacant space in your life. As far as I'm concerned, every second of uncertainty and every day spent longing for more was worth the wait, so long as we find ourselves here in the end.

THE END.

Mac & Beckett's Playlist

"Rumor" by Lee Brice
"Mary's Song (Oh My My My)" by Taylor Swift
"Friends Don't" by Maddie & Tae
"We're Not Friends" by Ingrid Andress
"Is Yet," by Gracie Carol
"Growing Old With You" by Restless Road

Listen to the full playlist on Spotify.

Did you enjoy *Fall for Me*?
Please leave a review.

Note From the Author

In most of my books, I like to sprinkle in something from my life that I love. With this book, it was the Jake's Shake from The Milkshake Factory. And of course, five months before *Fall for Me's* scheduled publication, Jake Guentzel was traded from the Pittsburgh Penguins and the Milkshake Factory discontinued the drink under that name. Instead of changing it to its new name (Cookie Brownie Fudge), I decided to leave it as a tribute to the first milkshake I ever tried and my love for the Penguins. And seriously, if you've never tasted this milkshake, you need to take a road trip to your nearest Milkshake Factory. Like yesterday.

RIP Jake's Shake. You will be missed.

In the meantime, go get yourself the newly renamed Cookie Brownie Fudge milkshake. You can thank me later ;)

P.S. This message is in no way sponsored—I just really love that milkshake.

Also by Lexi Kingston

13 Days of December

Remember December

Endure May

Trusting November

Forever June

Standalone Books

Fall for Me

If you're interested in paranormal romance, explore my other titles under Lexi J. Kingston:

Nightfall

Come Nightfall

In the Moonlight

Until Daybreak

After Sunrise

About the Author

Contemporary romance author Lexi Kingston started writing when she was fifteen years old solely because she was obsessed with the idea of creating fictional worlds like the ones she lived through growing up. There was this thrilling allure to writing characters that you can relate to and find pieces of yourself within that she couldn't shake, and this eventually drew her to fiction writing. She wanted to create a world people could get lost in—a fictional safe haven, if you will. A place filled with endless possibilities, where you can lose yourself, yet find yourself within the pages.

Lexi's paranormal romance titles are written under "Lexi J. Kingston."

LEXI KINGSTON ONLINE:
INSTAGRAM: @l.kingston.books
FACEBOOK: fb.me/l.kingston.books
TIKTOK: @l.kingston.books
TWITTER: @Lkingston_books
GOODREADS: goodreads.com/lkingstonbooks
BOOKBUB: bookbub.com/profile/lexi-kingston
WEBSITE: https://lkingstonbooks.com

Made in United States
Troutdale, OR
10/27/2024

24181248R00156